# Book of Dreams

# Also by Jon Konrath

Fiction:

The Failure Cascade (2020)

Ranch: The Musical (2019)

Help Me Find My Car Keys And We Can Drive Out! (2017)

Vol. 13 (2016)

He (2015)

The Memory Hunter (2014)

Atmospheres (2014)

Thunderbird (2013)

Sleep Has No Master (2012)

The Earworm Inception (2012)

Fistful of Pizza (2011)

Rumored to Exist (2002)

Summer Rain (2000)

Nonfiction:

The Necrokonicon (2006)

Dealer Wins (2004)

Tell Me a Story About the Devil (2003)

# Book of Dreams

Jon Konrath

Paragraph Line Books
Oakland, CA
www.paragraphline.com

For more information, visit www.rumored.com.

Cover art by Casey Babb (www.breakingbabb.com)

ISBN-13: 978-1-942086-11-6

PL-123 (v2)

I'm on a beach in Monterey. My left ear is bleeding for some reason, and I'm dabbing the blood with a baseball scorecard from the April 17, 2008 22-inning game between the San Diego Padres and the Colorado Rockies. David Lynch is at a John Steinbeck-themed hot dog stand, eating an *East of Eden* corn dog. I recognize him because of the trademark white hair, but he's almost incognito, wearing an oversized *Speed Racer* t-shirt and a pair of jorts that highlight his pale, spindly legs. He's barefoot, his feet stuck in the hot sand of the beach.

He's explaining the concept of Easter to a six-year-old Iranian girl. "...And there's this big bunny, see... and he nails this guy to a cross. Then he gives you marshmallows..." He tells me that Dalai Lama/hot dog/"make me one with everything" joke, and I pretend to laugh. I want to tell him about how my uncle learned how to meditate with a Tony Robbins tape before getting sent to prison, but I don't want to have to tell the story about how he got locked up for twenty years for trying to have sex with a Conrail locomotive.

I watch Lynch eat six corn dogs with nothing on them, then we go to the aquarium to buy a piece of the Berlin Wall encased in a solidified chunk of whale fat. "I don't think dolphins are real, bucko," he tells me.

\* \* \*

At a North Vietnamese military museum somewhere in central Illinois — the weird, dead part of the state way south of Peoria. I stopped to use the restroom and maybe get some nachos. I'm perplexed by the pro-Viet Cong cultural center in the middle of farm country. The cashier in the gift store has hair like the Bride of Frankenstein, with white streaks running up the sides. She talks like a Quaalude addict, keeps calling me "maaaaan" and tries to get me to buy a fried corn bread dish of some sort. I ask her if it's alcoholic, and she says, "Why not?"

The inside of the museum is hotter than it is outside in the July sun, due to an inefficient roof design and the use of a swamp cooler in an area with 100% humidity. The museum also uses walls of old tube TVs that are basically space heaters. I look at the dim displays playing faded videotapes of Jane Fonda workout videos, then examine the crashed remains of airplanes and burned-out tanks until I'm about to pass out from the heat. I go to the parking lot to rehydrate, but all I have in the car is coffee. I normally don't drink hot beverages, and the temperature is way too extreme outside to enjoy a scalding-hot drink. But I'd bought a box of Dunkin' Donuts coffee and don't want to throw it out. It's in a baby seat in the back of my vehicle, broiling away in the concentrated heat. I remember reading an article that drinking ten cups of coffee a day makes you live twice as long, but I'm not sure if it was a study paid for by Maxwell House or Starbucks.

Later that night, I'm in bed at a Hyatt Regency, reading articles about EZ-Pass, I-Pass, and the other largely incompatible electronic toll collection technologies in the United States. I'm convinced there's a possibility for arbitrage between the different systems that have reciprocity with the others. Some also give you free credit for new transponder purchases. I'm doing the math, and can't find a way to profit, but I'm sure there's an angle somewhere.

The phone rings, and someone is yelling at me in German. I fire up the Google Translate app to decrypt their nonsense. They're trying to tell me my great-grandfather owes $377 to Sprint PCS for a canceled cell phone contract. I explain that he died in 1881 in Austria, but they won't buy it, and keep asking for a credit card. Or maybe they speak a German dialect not supported by the translation app, and I'm missing something. I tell them to send a bill to the address for the Sears tower on South Wacker Drive, but they keep spelling it "Whacker." I eventually hang up and eat a fifty-dollar Toblerone bar from the hotel room minibar in one bite.

* * *

I'm working at a horrible company that does tech support for a septic tank self-care app. It involves twenty-hour shifts, seven days a week, and no lunch breaks. The HR department started a monthly raffle to boost morale after one of the employees died at his desk from dehydration. I win the contest, and the prize gives me three wishes. People normally use the wishes to get a new laptop, a pizza party, or Hawaiian shirt day on a Friday. I use mine to get three managers extradited to North Korea for war crimes.

\* \* \*

...In the parking garage of the SeaTac airport — I'm talking to a guy in a Greedo t-shirt and cowboy boots. I know that at some point in his life, he's owned a trench coat for aesthetic purposes. His orange Toyota Celica GT is parked across all three handicapped parking spots in the front row by the elevators. It's got a stereo with a subwoofer bigger around than a car tire in the trunk, the amps lit up with blue neon tubes. He's rocking the second Tori Amos album at a near-lethal volume.

The dude's trying to explain the store Hot Topic to me. I guess this is before I knew Hot Topic existed, or I'd only lived in parts of the country that had nothing edgier than an Ames department store. He could have just said "Spencer's for millennials," but instead, he's describing row-by-row, top-to-bottom every item in the store. I promise him I would check it out later, maybe buy a Misfits t-shirt for $50, but he keeps talking for another hour.

Inside, I meet Martha Stewart in the baggage area. I'm supposed to give her a ride to the Denny's by Northgate Mall. She's wearing sweats and a sweatshirt with a logo for the Indianapolis 500 on it, and not wearing any makeup. She tells me about a Sizzler restaurant in Tacoma that has shower facilities and spa treatments, available at an extra charge if you buy the buffet ticket. But I'm supposed to bring her to Denny's, and I tell her she can go to Sizzler later.

We wait for 45 minutes and her luggage does not show up on the conveyor. She tells me she checked a set of golf clubs and her deer rifle, along with a suitcase full of pills she needs immediately. A guy dressed in a British cop uniform tells us the bags are still in New Jersey because a U2 concert delayed every flight in the air. He starts singing an a cappella version of the song "Acrobat" from their *Achtung Baby* album, and we leave, without the bags. The parking machine charges me $647. I put it on a company Amex and hope I can expense it.

Later, I'm in a virtual reality game place in the mall. It used to be an abacus store, when those were briefly the hipster thing to have. After that fad passed, the owner still had ten months left on his lease, so he got a half-dozen video goggle setups and a fleet of old Commodore Amiga computers. The proprietor, a faded punk rock-looking guy with thick glasses and horrible teeth, explains to me every minute detail of the Amiga add-on boards and expanders while two hyperactive kids with goggles strapped to their heads wave their hands in the air. They look like hamsters trying to climb out of their aquarium cage.

I want to try the game, but I'm afraid of getting ringworm from the goggles, even though he wipes them with vodka after each session. He tells me that the Elder-Beerman store in the mall is selling a cologne that smells exactly like a Volkswagen Rabbit with a diesel engine. I think about buying some and spraying down the interior of my car for nostalgic purposes, but car air fresheners tend to give me headaches and asthma.

I go to the department store anyway, and Martha Stewart is there, working at the fragrance counter, but she's now dressed in expensive business attire and steampunk-looking welding goggles. She offers me a free gym bag if I buy any four Calvin Klein aftershaves, but I do the math, and it's not worth it. I tell her about how I used to have a nude photo of Kate Moss in my apartment, a full-page ad cut out of a *Details* magazine. She laughs and tells me *Details* is for men who don't know they're gay yet. I'm pretty sure someone else said that quote first (Bret Easton Ellis?) I tell her I just started reading the magazine because Joe Rogan was on the cover. "I rest my case," she says.

\* \* \*

The Manpower temp agency gets me a gig making a Dungeons and Dragons module with Imelda Marcos and Guy Fieri. Marcos is doing the artwork — I never knew she was an accomplished painter of fantasy creatures, but she did a bunch of custom vans with wizards and dragons and warlocks back in the Seventies, and she's credited with the artwork for a gatefold album cover for the band Yes. (Maybe it was for Anderson/Bruford/Wakeman/Howe — I'm not a big Yes fan, I honestly can't stand Jon Anderson's singing.) Fieri is supposed to be adding recipes for the module, and I'm writing the actual text, drawing the maps, and doing the layout in PageMaker.

Guy Fieri keeps arguing with me in Google Chat about the cartography details of the maps for each level, and he starts every argument with "I TOOK A THREE-CREDIT GEOGRAPHY CLASS AT UNLV – I KNOW WHAT I AM TALKING ABOUT." I tell him, "You stick with the fucking loaded tater tot nachos, this is my vision." Imelda doesn't know how to use a computer, and FedExes polaroids of her paintings. She works in acrylics on chunks of unprimed drywall instead of canvas and it all looks horrible.

After a year of going back and forth with little progress, Gary Gygax threatens to sue us. He doesn't even own TSR anymore (I didn't even know he was *alive* anymore), but tales of Fieri's antics go viral, and everyone is posting "I KNOW CARTOGRAPHY" memes online. TSR stock is plummeting, and they threaten to call the National Guard to stop us. I think I quit the project, or get fired, and Judith Regan hires a ghostwriter to finish my work.

\* \* \*

I drive to the middle of Iowa where they are holding an atmospheric hydrogen bomb test. Pixar paid the government a few million dollars to light off an H-bomb so they could digitize the footage and use it in a cartoon about anorexic mermaids who overcame dyslexia. Tickets cost $68 to watch the event from about five miles away, plus food and drink. There are VIP seats that were closer, but you have to know someone, or have cancer or something.

They seat everyone in metal bleachers, like a high school football game, but without a marching band. No outside food is allowed, but concession stands sell "atomic dogs" and cans of Pepsi. The "atomic" doesn't mean anything — they are probably from Sam's Club, microwaved. I snuck in a blue Powerade in my camera bag, but am afraid to drink it and get busted.

A public affairs officer from a nearby military base is reading a list of rules while his assistant passes out floppy plastic sunglasses like the ones they give you for free at the optometrist when you get your eyes dilated for no reason. "DO NOT LOOK AT THE BLAST! DO NOT LOOK AT THE BLAST! DO NOT LOOK AT THE BLAST! AND NO PHOTOGRAPHY! ABSOLUTELY NO PHOTOGRAPHY!" I absolutely knew everyone was going to look directly into the blast and burn out their retinas while taking selfies.

The family sitting next to me has a kid with a bowl haircut playing a banjo who keeps singing the song from the Vonage commercial, that "woo-hoo, woo-hoo-hoo" song. I want to throttle him, but I don't want to get some kind of federal assault charge because we're on an official Department of Energy test site. It also takes two hands to hold my wobbly cardboard tray of hot dogs and soggy microwave french fries, and if I drop it, that's $47 down the drain.

They play "The Final Countdown" through the shitty sound system. The blast goes off and is underwhelming because we're so far away. I expect the sky to fill with a giant mushroom cloud of smoke brighter than the sun, but it looks like a quick ball of light and a distant puff of smoke on the horizon, then the usual amount of smoggy blackness you'd see on any given day in Gary, Indiana by the steel mills. A minute later, the sonic wave reaches us and vibrates the aluminum bleachers like a washboard being played by a hillbilly at a country music show.

I wear the plastic glasses all day and try to convince people at the mall that I'm a member of Devo, but nobody believes me because I don't have the helmet or the plastic radiation suit.

* * *

The parking lot of a deer petting zoo — a fat Mexican guy in a Wonder Woman costume is trying to asphyxiate himself in a first-generation Prius, the goofy-looking model that looks like a bootleg aqua blue Toyota Echo. He has a rubber hose running from the exhaust pipe to the sunroof, but it's in EV mode so nothing is happening. I tap on his window and yell at him to check his VIN number online to see if the car was affected by the Takata airbag recall, because the Toyota dealer would replace their airbags at no cost, but you have to book a repair appointment very far in advance.

His stereo is on too loud and he can't hear me. He's listening to an old Styx album (*Cornerstone*, I think) at top volume. The guy who played strings on that album was also in Mannheim Steamroller, and I remember a Christmas decades before when I was obsessed with both the Mannheim Steamroller holiday album and Drakkar cologne, which made me start thinking about asphyxiating myself.

The guy suddenly wakes up during the song "Babe" and drives away at top speed, about thirty-seven miles an hour. I buy a corn dog and try to feed it to a deer, but the park ranger, who looks like an overweight Eddie Vedder, says they're all vegan now.

\* \* \*

At an actuarial sciences conference in San Diego... I'm sharing a hotel room with Michael Jordan. I want to go to Denny's, but Jordan's in a battle with the front desk because his bed is not long enough. He's arguing with them to bring up a cot and put it at the end of his twin bed so it's long enough for him, but I know that won't work because the footboard of the bed would get in the way. He insists the bed/footboard situation could be fixed with a ramp of pillows. He also wants a hamburger, and a formal apology in writing, which I know will never happen. I tell MJ I need to leave before Denny's closes, even though it is open 24/7.

The rental car is a garbage subcompact Pontiac with a tough-guy name like Fire or Bro or Gun, and something is wrong with the brakes; they continually make a grinding or squealing sound and smell like burning asbestos. I drive to a Borders bookstore, and Henry Rollins is doing a promo for his new country/western album he did with half the guys from Slayer. I ask him to sign a copy of a James Patterson book, and he punches me in the head and tells me to buy his fucking album, because it's got a cover of "Diamonds and Rust" on it. I ask if it's the Joan Baez or the Judas Priest version, and he says it's both. I buy a CD, but then when I get back to my car in the parking lot, it only has a MiniDisc player in it.

When I finally get to the Denny's, a big group of people from my job (but not Michael Jordan) are attempting to order fancy French food off-menu. Janice from accounting is mansplaining to a Mexican fry cook with a teardrop prison tattoo how to cook the Julia Childs recipe for coq au vin. I hide from everyone in a back corner, order my usual Moons Over My Hammy, and try to talk to someone on the Mir space station with a small ham radio, but then remember I can't speak any Russian.

* * *

A Shoney's restaurant, in London — I'm eating a box of cherry Pop-Tarts, and crumbs are flying everywhere. They've opened a chain of the diners in the UK for American nostalgia reasons, but they're all located in high-rise office buildings with modern, all-glass architecture. The place has none of the country kitchen charm or kitsch, and the food isn't right at all: wrong cuts of bacon, wrong color of eggs, blood sausage instead of Jimmy Deans, sides of beans and fried tomatoes for some damn reason.

I'm on vacation, but trying to catch up on work emails on an old Compaq luggable laptop that's as big as a suitcase and weighs two hundred pounds. A manager at our Vang Vieng campus in Laos drowned in a dunk tank at a work party, and there are a thousand reply-to-all messages offering thoughts and prayers and/or trying to get his corner office. I'm deleting the messages as fast as possible, and know I'm going to get assigned all of his work and have to fly home early.

A kid who looks like he's about ten and talks in an Oliver Twist accent asks me why I voted for the Elephant Man. He's playing with a laminated map of Moscow that must have been printed thirty years ago. I tell him I like John Hurt's work, and support John Merrick's economic platform, then start eating the Pop-Tarts two at a time, hoping a cop wouldn't show up to deport me.

* * *

Anchorage, Alaska — it's eleven at night, and completely daylight out, so it must be in June or July. I'm in the parking lot of a Burger King across from a strip mall, and a guy in a Marines uniform is telling me that if I sign up for twenty years, I get a free clarinet. I'm eating a BK burrito, which has ground-up chunks of Whopper meat in it. I tell him I have a long history of mental illness, and he says, "Just make sure not to tell the doctors. Don't even tell them your real name." I try to negotiate with the recruiter, ask for a tuba or a signing bonus. He offers to buy me a Whaler sandwich. I pass.

I cross the street, go to a used book shop. Inside, I can tell it used to be a low-end department store or garden center, like maybe a Big R discount place. It still smells faintly like fertilizer and pesticide. I search for my own name in the fiction section, and they have a dozen books written by me that I do not recognize at all, weird titles and covers that look like they were printed by a freak underground press in the Seventies.

A book I allegedly wrote is titled *It's Not Cheating If You're Dead*. I flip to a random page, and it describes the scene that just happened with the guy in the Marine uniform, except it also had a long riff about how he thought he was addicted to pornography because he had two subscriptions to *Penthouse* magazine, one for home and one for the office. I'm not sure if the alternate universe me who wrote the book embellished this, or if that timeline was slightly different.

I'd also written a book about growing corn and various herbs at high latitudes, and what lights to use to stretch out the growing season. I know nothing about gardening, and make a note to check out my writing on the subject later. I try to buy my books, but the cashier checks my ID and says it's a violation of the Nielsen Amendment, and I could go to federal prison for two years for trying to jack up my BookScan numbers.

* * *

My neighbor collected his urine for a year and put it in a transparent plastic 1:10 scale model of a 737 jet in his back yard. It looks like the Wonder Woman invisible jet, but filled with bright gold liquid. He claims it is an art project, something about urban decay after the Boeing Bust in Seattle in 1971. "If you can write a good enough artist's statement," he tells me, "you can shit in a box and become a millionaire."

His neighbor on the other side, a guy who delivers pizzas for a living, is mowing his yard and hits an English walnut sitting on the ground under one of his neglected fruit trees. The shrapnel from the nut's hard shell flies out of the mower like a bullet and goes straight through the plastic jet next door. Piss leaks everywhere and smelled for weeks. The city comes out and sandbags the guy's yard, so it won't flood the road and block traffic.

Someone from the neighborhood homeowners' association came to my door while I'm asleep, trying to get me to sign a petition so they can sue somebody for negligence, but I don't remember if they are suing the guy with the jet, the guy with the mower, or maybe Toro for making the mower and not putting a warning sticker on it.

* * *

In Vegas... At the grave of Wayne Newton with a guy who lost all his money betting against the Harlem Globetrotters. He's an old college buddy, from the semester I spent trying to be a postmodern weatherman. He owns a chain of check cashing places in Kansas or Nebraska, and keeps saying his wife is going to kill him when she finds out about the lost bet, and he needs to kill himself first, which makes no sense, unless he really wants to make sure his wife doesn't go to jail, and he'd be dead anyway, so why bother.

We pour Metamucil onto Newton's grave, and it's 118 degrees outside, so it sizzles and fries into an orange caramel sauce. Even though we're nauseous from the heat, we find a restaurant that serves Cambodian/Nazi German fusion food. The lunch is borderline inedible, but the joint has no waiting list and good air conditioning. At the table, we gorge on bread and he tells me he's thinking of killing himself on the roller coaster at the New York, New York casino, and if his body hits the fake United Nations building, he'll get diplomatic immunity. I tell him the jump is not possible because of centrifugal force, and they replaced that UN with a Duane Reade drug store. He says, "Thanks a lot for shitting in my soup, Mr. Wizard," and throws his food on the floor.

Back at the Excalibur, I get the hotel doctor from the concierge desk to inject him with Demerol before he hurts himself or others. As he's crying and drifting into a drug stupor, I ask him to tell me the exact amount he wagered on the game, thinking it was some outrageous sum, in the hundreds of thousands of dollars. It turns out he only lost $49, but his wife is Mennonite or Mormon or something and will leave him for even placing a bet.

Later, I'm at a Cirque du Soleil-themed public execution at the Circus Circus, where a bunch of French clowns or acrobats or whatever are giving lethal injections to various federal prisoners. It's a comp ticket — no way I'd pay for something like this. But I feel like I had to at least go until the first intermission.

* * *

I'm on an ambivalent first date with a biology major. We meet at a restaurant where they serve microwave tortillas and TV dinners on wooden chess boards. The Summer Olympics is in some distant Asian country that just changed names or went through a revolution, and nobody really knows where it is. They are maybe twelve or fourteen hours earlier or later, and the broadcast isn't time-delayed. Bars and restaurants are staying open all night so people can watch pole vaulting semifinals at three in the morning.

The woman is attractive, but can't have a five-minute conversation without mentioning the Svalbard global seed vault at least ten times. She has an unnatural obsession with the bunker dug deep into a mountain on a remote Norwegian island and keeps talking about how she wants to work there someday. I imagine this would involve some ungodly commute, like flying in a seaplane for thousands of vomit-inducing miles in arctic storms every week, or maybe spending six-month shifts in an underground dormitory, going Jack Torrance from the total isolation.

I keep trying to change the topic — local news, fun facts about vintage airplane engines, sports scores, sex talk — nothing works. It always comes back to that vault of seeds. I only vaguely know about the Olympics, and try to steer the conversation back there, but keep failing, and then start worrying that she thinks I was one of those people who actually gave a fuck about the Olympics, which is even worse.

There's an involved argument about who will pay for the food, and we end up splitting the check 90/10, because I weigh more. I go home alone and watch a TV movie about a Latvian kid addicted to granola bars.

* * *

I'm talking with Owen Wilson at the design-a-kitchen center in Home Depot. He's wearing the orange employee apron with no shirt underneath and sweats profusely. His body has the odor of a diesel-powered submarine twenty days into a month-long cruise, and his skin is gray like an unembalmed corpse.

I went to the store to ask how to sharpen one of those flat carpenter's pencils, because it won't fit in a standard crank-operated sharpener. I think maybe there's a trick other than carefully carving away the wood with a pocket knife and slicing open my fingers ten times, but it turns out there isn't.

He wants me to eat a quart of warm Miracle Whip from a Yankee Stadium 40th anniversary commemorative mini-helmet in the parking lot of an Arco station in Clearwater, Florida. I can't remember if Miracle Whip is the one that doesn't go bad at room temperature because it isn't real mayonnaise. He drags me out to the Mexican hot dog stand in front of the store, and shows me a plastic bin filled with individually wrapped packets of Miracle Whip, or maybe Hellman's, all at room temperature. "What the hell? Nobody's dying out here!"

I wonder if the botulism only happens when you expose a container to oxygen, like those rocket fuels that light off when exposed to air. All I really know was that I need a hot dog with mayo on it, and a root beer, maybe some chips. I look in my wallet to see if I can cover a meal deal, but I've only got Yugoslavian money and a club card to Lucky's grocery store, so I leave.

* * *

I'm digging through piles of rotting, waterlogged paperback books at a general store by a marina. Half the books are completely drenched, dripping wet, pages stuck together. They fall apart when I try to flip through them, like trying to read a pile of wet leaves. The books remind me of the dirty magazines we used to find in the woods when we were kids. I can't recognize any of the titles in the store, all by unknown authors. I don't know if I'm just not that well-read, or if these were all flash-in-the-pan pulp writers of the Fifties, total unknowns.

The shopkeeper is a woman who looks a hundred and fifty years old, eyes sunken deep into a face that resembles the texture of dried fruit. Her flesh has the same consistency as a shrunken head. She's sitting at a semicircular desk covered in piles of books, magazines, and faded computer printouts. An obsolete Apple II buzzes away in front of her, its orange-screen monitor displaying a crude pornographic hangman game. She yells at her cats about comparative religion and ignores me. She's missing both legs, and I really want to ask her how that happened, but I know nothing good can come of it.

There's a big self-surgery section, and I dig through all the manuals, trying to find something that isn't badly damaged, anything that might be interesting at all. I feel like I need to buy a book or two to support the store, but there's nothing I could find that, even if it was handed to me for free, I wouldn't immediately throw in the garbage. It also doesn't help that the entire store is lit by a single forty-watt bulb and has no windows, so I can barely see in front of my face. I give up, look for an exit, a way to sneak out without the woman seeing me.

I find a hidden door in the back of the store that goes into an Irish bar, so I slide out, sit at the counter of the tavern, eat the free soda bread. I put five pats of butter on each little piece of the stiff, crumbly bread. I can't remember if it's butter or margarine that is bad for you, but I suppose eating twenty packets in a row of either one is probably not good.

A waitress who looks like Minnie Driver watches me, impressed by how much churned fat I can eat. I think about asking her out, but then remember a picture I saw in the *National Enquirer* of Minnie Driver smoking a cigar at a gas pump and decide it's probably for the best that I die alone.

\* \* \*

A man who looks like Ho Chi Minh in a leisure suit is lecturing me about how I'm pushing my cart through Kmart. He has some insane theory that one should push a cart under-handed, to reduce tendon damage. He keeps grabbing my cart out of my hands and shrieking in Vietnamese, while showing me how to push it (the wrong way) like I was a five year old who had just shit on the floor.

It reminds me of my old roommate from Spain, a trombone prodigy who would later get deported for shoplifting bras. He always insisted one should wash their hands and dishes in cold water to kill germs. He used to bang on my door for hours because he had perfect pitch and I constantly listened to atonal experimental synthesizer music that semester, and the impure musical notes drove him insane. He also got dysentery from his dirty plates, but still insisted I was wrong, then played horrible baroque music on the trombone for hours before going to Target to steal women's underwear.

I want to buy a discount FEMA trailer at the Kmart, but end up looking at fertilizer bags for hours, wondering if a green lawn would make me feel more complete as a person. I go to the Big K Cafe to get some corn dogs and crinkle-cut fries. Their Icee machine is broken, and they don't have Big K soda on draft (why not?) so I order a regular fountain Coke with my corn dog meal deal. A hipster couple with ironic hair make out in the back of the cafeteria, a sloppy display of public affection. They smell like death. It is the anniversary of 9/11 and all the TVs in the cafe show loops of the plane crashes and collapsing towers, over and over. I eat the corn dogs fast, then leave without buying anything else.

\* \* \*

A Mexican news channel is playing on the TV set in the Greek diner. I want a salad with feta on it because of a David Bowie documentary I watched the night before. The news show talks about a group of kids who killed their neighbor because of a comic book, but I don't speak Spanish, and I'm too lazy to read subtitles. I'm wearing a bulletproof vest, which makes me sweat profusely under its plastic lining, even though it's cold and rainy out. The inside of the diner feels like a sauna, the humidity swirling around the interior.

The waitress brings over a bowl full of cheese chunks covered in a golden syrupy liquid and says it would help my heatstroke. I eat the concoction with a small wooden spoon, and it makes me think about being in the Appalachian mountains twenty years before. I was doing standup comedy at a vegan beer house, and nobody was listening, because Kennedy from MTV had been shot. Everyone huddled around an old wooden Philco radio and listened to a scratchy AM station for further updates. I did a joke about autoerotic asphyxiation, but nobody heard the punch line.

The cheese-syrup mixture is making me sleepy, and I suddenly recognize the taste — it's codeine cough syrup. It pairs well with the feta, except for the horrible aftertaste. I order a turkey sandwich to go, then walk to Burger Master so I can eat the sandwich with a side of their french fries. The manager won't let me in with outside food, so I throw out the sandwich, order some curly fries instead. Inside, a group of street dancers are rhythmically swaying to a song from Sting's 1999 album *Brand New Day*, which is being played over the store intercom.

* * *

I call the Microsoft Visual Studio support line claiming I'd been abducted by a group of time-traveling aliens and had an MSVC conflict error. The customer support representative, who sounds like an Irish hooligan from a bad cop show, asks me twenty questions about my registration and warranty information and Microsoft Live ID, and I proceed to read him the ingredients list from the back of a Lean Cuisine dinner several times. He tells me I need to install the latest .NET update and hangs up on me. An hour later, a robot calls me and asks me to rate my experience, and I tell it the support guy killed my parents in the name of Satan.

* * *

The heat and hot water is out in my apartment. The boiler exploded in the middle of the night, and luckily nobody was killed by the flying shrapnel. I'm bathing myself in the kitchen by drenching paper towels with denatured isopropyl alcohol and rubbing them on my body. I suddenly remember that a Soviet Cosmonaut burned to death in a training accident doing this when the pure alcohol lit on fire in a 100% oxygen pressure chamber from a heating pad or some electrical sparks. Right as I remember this, my doorbell rings, and I freak out, thinking it will cause an ambient electrical spark and kill me.

At the door, one of my neighbors says he's starting a rent strike over the busted water boiler, and he wants to pool the money and buy the Jumbotron screen from Shea Stadium, which was getting torn down to build that Bernie Madoff piece of shit. I don't know where he thinks he can put the video scoreboard, but I instantly get upset at him, because it would probably end up in front of my apartment, and blind me with light and video replays day and night. Also, I hate the Mets.

I'm about to tell him to go screw, but my landlord shows up, tells everyone to cut the shit with the rent strike. He looks exactly like Marlon Brando in *The Godfather*. He mumbles something about how he will fix the boiler with duct tape after it goes on sale at Kmart. But he's eating an orange, so I know he's about to get killed. I go back in the apartment, hide in my bathtub and wait for gunshots and the Nino Rota music cue that always gets played when a gangster gets shot.

\* \* \*

I'm unloading boxes from a forty-foot trailer on a department store loading dock, looking for a crate of limited-edition Van Halen CDs that are part of a promotion, because I know I could sell them for a hundred bucks each. David Lee Roth also works there. He is no longer with the band — this is after Sammy Hagar, after Gary Cherone, when Danny Bonaduce briefly sang for them. Diamond Dave isn't being that helpful with the unload, and keeps practicing ninja movies with a broom, yelling nonsensical lines like "if it had not been for the laws of this land, I would have destroyed all of you!"

When I finish my shift and go outside, the sun is just starting to rise. The exterior of the store is made from the brownish-red lava rock briquettes they put inside gas barbecue ovens and fake fireplaces, and I can feel the heat radiating from the building like I'm standing next to a bonfire. I remember a drunken helicopter pilot telling me about a world record where the temperature in Montana changed by a hundred degrees in a day, going from negative-60 to 60 degrees Fahrenheit. I wanted to tell him that was really a 120-degree change, but he was flying the chopper, and pretty distracted and drunk already, and I didn't want us to crash.

The Meat Puppets are busking in front of a First National bank next to the store. The drummer, who is wearing KISS face paint, has set up his kit inside the glass ATM building like it was an isolation booth. They are jamming out the song "Slow Ride" by Foghat for like twenty minutes, playing the "slow ride / take it easy" line from the chorus over and over. Most passers-by do not pay any attention to them. An old man with white hair and gigantic hearing aids stumbles past with his hands over his ears, screaming in anguish.

The band takes a break to drink a case of warm Big Red soda. I go to a Kroger grocery store across the street with their bassist Cris Kirkwood, so we can get more generic cream soda. He tells me if you put a stick of white Wrigley's chewing gum in a banana and wrap it with tin foil, you could eat it a week later and trip balls. I think it's an urban legend, but I don't say anything, because he's got a record deal and I don't. I ask him why my JC Penney bass guitar sounds so bad, and he tells me I should get it re-fretted, even though it is only like three months old.

When I get home, I have exactly two hours to sleep until I have to report to a government facility and register for the draft. My eyes are really red, and I'm afraid they will arrest me for being stoned. I put in this new eye drop that came free in the new issue of *Reader's Digest*. It's a blue liquid that looks like the berry punch variety of Fla-vor-ice pops, the juice in the long, clear plastic tube you freeze overnight. The drops cause a cool sensation to flow through my entire body, from my eyes down to my toes. I then read the package and find out they are made of pure opium.

I read a newspaper on the drive to the exam. A local doctor was arrested for trying to transplant a dog's head onto a first-grade teacher, in order to keep her alive forever. It didn't kill her, and the procedure itself wasn't technically illegal; the lawsuit was over predatory advertising practices and if her teacher's license was still valid.

\* \* \*

At a place near Penn Station... it looks like a buffet restaurant or a grocery store deli, but the stainless steel bins at the steam table are filled with cadaver parts and plumbing supplies. I dig through a pan full of eyeballs, not really looking for a particular color, just enjoying the texture. Then I rummage through a few trays of greasy plastic pipe fittings, elbows and tees, before leaving the line and jumping behind the counter to vomit in a dish sink.

A woman with the bangs of a creative writing adjunct professor gives me attitude about being sick, maybe thinking I work there and had to wash my hands after vomiting. I ignore her, and tell a dishwasher with a peach fuzz mustache that I thought the Chevrolet Monte Carlo was a mistake bigger than the Ford Pinto, and it only proved that someone at GM drank too much Coca-Cola. I forget what my line of reasoning was, but it upset the kid, and he started crying, so I leave.

* * *

There is an earthquake in the middle of Indiana. I'm at the mall, and we're evacuated in the basement of a Target, which I didn't even know had a basement. Also, I thought you only did that for tornados and nuclear war, not earthquakes. A meathead guy with a crew cut keeps telling me how the earthquake started at the exact same second he punched his kid in the face, and for just a second, he thought he caused it. Someone in a red Target vest is handing out little paper cups of fluoride, in minty green flavor, so our teeth won't rot from liquefaction. "If this was a real attack, we should all remove our spleens and gall bladders," says an old-timey guy with white hair in a lab coat. "It's what they'll do for the alleged Mars missions, if they ever fund them."

After the all-clear siren, I go to a local diner-and-burgers place to meet with a girl I'd once been trying to set my friend up with. She's with a new boyfriend that rebuilds tractor engines ironically and is obsessed with craft beer. I order a crispy chicken sandwich with gouda cheese on it, which is probably the most exotic cheese I'd ever tried. It reminds me of when I had my wisdom teeth pulled and could only eat cheese and Ensure shakes for a month. I got whacked out on pain pills for a week straight and did nothing but watch Meg Ryan movies and shovel down thin slices of Velveeta I had to chew with my front teeth.

At the diner, I notice the girl's bleach-blonde hair has a tinge of green to it. She is talking nonstop about her ideas and extrapolations on *Twin Peaks*, which just came out. Her theory is that the show has to do with the Armenian genocide, but I don't understand her reasoning. (It has something to do with Leland Palmer looking like an Ottoman.) The hamburger is dripping hot oil down my arms, and I'm wiping my hands after every other bite with a Holiday Inn towel, but it isn't helping. I think I'll probably have to take a shower and burn my clothes by the time I finish lunch.

Outside, a group of graduate students are protesting the metric system in the parking lot of an AutoZone. I can't tell if they are pro- or anti-metric. I stop and talk to a guy on the way to my car, and he keeps saying he needs to buy a metric egg tray for Mother's day. Maybe a metric dozen eggs is like only ten, I don't know. I don't eat hardboiled eggs — every time I try to cook them, they turn into pure green botulism — so I just nod my head and act like I understood.

At my car, there is an orange envelope under the windshield wiper, and I'm pissed off that I somehow got a parking ticket for parking in a mall with no signs or meters or anything. When I get home, I'm still upset, but I open the envelope, and it contains a long-form review of the new Sepultura album. I already bought a copy of the album on CD, so I throw out the review, but keep the envelope to use for a future prank.

* * *

I've got six fingers on my one hand and four on the other. It's like my right pinky somehow ended up on my left hand. I don't know if I was born this way and never noticed it, or if the finger migrated overnight, like how teeth slowly drift into position when you put braces on them. I spend about an hour trying to move each finger separately to see if there are any interdependent tendons that would cause me to move multiple fingers at the same time, but everything seems to be wired well.

I realize it's going to be impossible for me to re-learn how to touch type or buy winter gloves. But I could probably learn some excellent guitar chords, like throw in an extra eleventh note on top of a jazz chord. (Not that I've done a good job of mastering any of the chords involving only five fingers.) I write a letter to Steve Vai and ask him if he has any video lessons on how to shred with six fingers. He writes back months later and tells me to never buy a radial arm saw online.

* * *

I'm watching the movie *Papillon* on a nine-inch black-and-white portable TV while an orthopedic surgeon who smells like bologna is doing an intra-articular injection of corticosteroids into my big toe. My entire foot is cherry-red from a massive gout attack, and the pain is so severe, I couldn't even think of putting on socks or shoes. I've been marathoning Tylenol-3 with codeine for days, with little effect. I had to push myself to the subway on a Tony Hawk skateboard I found at the Salvation Army.

I eat chunks of ginger candy, and think about making a casserole for dinner, but don't have anything at home in the fridge except single-serve condiments and bottles of sweetened iced tea, and I'm not in the mood to carry groceries on the subway. The doctor finishes the injection, and my gout-infested toe immediately feels cool and pain-free. I ask him if I'm okay to go to Strand books and buy a copy of the new Ayatollah Khomeini autobiography, and he tells me to swaddle my toes in silk and use a cane on the opposite side. He packs up his medical kit in a bowling ball case, and says he'd send me a bill on AOL.

I walk with a folding cane that has a blowgun in the barrel, go down a Chinatown alley to a pizza-by-the-slice place. (Strand is closed for a Satanic holiday.) They are roasting KFC chicken wings on a large wok, like from a Mongolian barbecue restaurant. The Italian cook is talking about how he was going to get LASIK surgery, because Tiger Woods got it, and he depends on his eyesight to make millions of dollars. I want to order a deep-dish pizza, but I'm in New York and don't want to get shot.

* * *

Everyone at my job has gastric bypass surgery over the weekend, and I get worried that I missed an email, because I didn't hear anything about it until everyone rolls in on Monday morning, full of stitches and staples, sipping protein shakes an ounce at a time and popping fentanyl every hour. I wonder if I need to rush out and get a lap band installed just to keep my job.

This is in the middle of Kansas or Iowa in the early Nineties, when weight loss surgery is rare. I think I saw it on TV once, but never knew anyone who had it done, and now everyone in my department is missing ninety percent of their stomach. Even the borderline anorexic admin assistant who works the front desk got sliced from stem to stern and had her entire digestive system removed. I go to my cube and try to figure out how many personal items I can stuff in my backpack in case I get escorted out by security.

There's a taco truck that parks out front every morning, selling monster burritos that weigh five pounds each. When I sneak downstairs at noon for my usual taco plate, the owner and his wife are crying, and say they will go bankrupt if nobody in the company will eat anymore. I draw a complicated diagram on the back of a napkin, a new business plan, and when I wake up, I think I invented DoorDash in 1993.

* * *

In the parking lot of a dead mall... a guy's driving on his rims with shredded tires at fifty miles an hour and trying to shoot up liquid cocaine in his eyeball with a worn-out insulin needle he stole from a gas station bathroom's sharps container. I only know the details because Waylon Jennings is doing a voice-over in my head for some reason. The beat-up K-car hits a curb, jumps in the air sideways, and everything freeze frames for a second while Waylon says, "That boy's sure gonna have a hard time gettin' out of this one!"

The car lands on its side, rolls into a convenience store, but no police show up. The rapture is happening, so assorted people are floating to heaven, but a lot of them aren't. There's a church in about every fourth building in this town, and they're all filled with people who have cashed out their retirements and mortgages to hand over to preachers for eternal salvation. All of them still have fat asses in seats, not rising to heaven whatsoever.

I walk into the mall, and a guy with a *Three Stooges* bowl haircut is sitting at an ISIS recruiting booth, reading *Meth Lab Aficionado* magazine. I ask him if they have any free stuff, like hats or pens, and he says their revenue is really down because of the rapture thing. "I'm expecting a big up-swing once people realize they're screwed. If you've got no reason to go to church anymore, might as well start flying planes into buildings, right? Can I get you to sign up? I've got a box of keychains coming next week."

I go to a Wilson's Leather and buy an Andrew Dice Clay leather jacket with the huge shoulders, metal spikes all over it, and no sleeves. The back of it says "BRO JOB" in fake rhinestones, which I'm not that thrilled about, but it's fifty percent off, so why not. The salesperson looks like Bill Murray, and tells me he doesn't work on commission, and he can get me a deal on a leather gimp suit. He starts shimmering like he's a hologram in a bad science fiction movie, and I leave.

Outside, an armada of Harleys driven by a dentistry cult fill the highway in front of the mall, thousands of choppers to the horizon and beyond. A man in the shirt from a McDonald's uniform drenched in blood stands in front of an abandoned Payless Shoes, chanting "JORTS! JORTS! JORTS!" and pumping his fist in the air as the cult members zoom past on their motorcycles. He isn't wearing jorts — just a pair of Wrangler carpenter pants — but he appears to be an enthusiast. He turns to me and yells, "I AM MARS, THE GOD OF WAR, AND I WILL CUT YOU DOWN," right before he gets hit by a fat endodontist on a custom XR1200 with a naked lady painted on the gas tank.

\* \* \*

At a work picnic — they rented out an amusement park that only does corporate events. It has a roller coaster, a diseased swimming pool, and a few crap kiddie rides. There's always a lot of junk food, and they're giving away a chrome-plated AR-15 with a sniper scope in a raffle.

The daughter of a project manager is there, in a plastic bubble with oxygen tanks. She had been in a car accident in an old Ford Pinto, and 95% of her skin was boiled away by burning gasoline. The girl is about my age, and used to be very physically attractive, like a cheerleader type, but now she's missing her arms and legs, and her remaining skin is glossy and blackened, like a bad rotisserie chicken.

Everyone's talking to her and saying she's so brave, or complimenting her on how she looks, pretending nothing is wrong. But I remember before the accident, she was petty and bitchy. Like one time, my friend Gordon asked her out, and she made him buy her five Cabbage Patch kids — this was a Christmas when it was impossible to buy one, let alone five — and when he somehow bought them at an incredible premium, she put them all into the garbage disposal, then told everyone in school that Gordon shit his pants because he was scared of *The Little Mermaid*. So I have mixed feelings about the whole thing.

My coworker Charlie and I wander through a promenade of crappy amusements, and find a row of old arcade games, including a classic Tetris machine. It's coin-op, but also issues strips of paper skee-ball tickets you can exchange for prizes, ejecting a ticket every time you cleared out a row. Nobody was playing the machine, because it cost money. Whoever set it up had obviously not calculated the payout situation, because we put in a quarter each and walk away with something like fifty million tickets, and the biggest prize at the ticket counter is a Harrier jump jet, which costs 10,000 tickets.

We eat double-fried corn dogs at a picnic table, and talk about the tax implications of the Tetris win, and if it would be possible to maybe trade the tickets for the entire amusement park. Charlie thinks it would pay out more if we sold all the rides and used the land to build a mini-mall or maybe a golf course. As we scheme and eat, the power goes out and the ice cream vendors start giving away their product. I eat four ice cream sandwiches, which are half liquid and end up making me puke on the Little Dipper ride.

\* \* \*

A guy is standing by the side of the road holding a sign that says "PLEASE GO FUCK YOURSELVES." I'm establishing telepathic communication with an Indian contortionist and eating a jar of pickled wolf ears in a borscht sauce from Vladivostok. The telepathy doesn't work 100%, because I'm distracted, can't focus. I'm pissed off at this girl I went to high school with. She had seven kids by seven dads and always posts on Facebook about the time she got finger blasted by Guy Fieri in the parking lot of a Ralph's grocery store on South Rancho Drive in Las Vegas. I know she's lying, because I maintain a comprehensive Guy Fieri wiki, and I have a list of every public appearance he's made, ever.

I go to an Aldi's grocery store, and a guy in the parking lot is selling a Persian rug of Ted Koppel's face. My nose is running a putrid green snot, so I don't talk to him. I go inside the store to buy a kleenex, and I find an Axe version of Depends undergarments for bros who are incontinent but are into extreme sports. I buy one and it smells like a cab driver. When I go back outside, the rug guy, who looks exactly like Charles Bukowski, is arguing with a nun, saying money orders do not exist.

* * *

I'm in an old dorm room: heavy wood trim, giant single-pane windows, Victorian-looking furniture, a real *Dead Poet's Society* vibe to it. I feel like I should be wearing a tweed jacket with patches on the elbows, drinking expensive Scotch, and planning a summer trip to Europe with my trust fund money. Instead, I'm sitting on a lumpy, narrow bed, eating from a five-pound bucket of Kroger crunchy peanut butter with my bare hands. I had some generic saltines, but finished my last sleeve hours ago, and can't find any clean silverware, so my hand is my spoon. The oil keeps separating from the peanut butter, so I have to periodically stir it with a wire coat hanger.

My roommate is tearing apart a Yamaha DX-7 synthesizer for an ethnomusicology project I don't understand. The innards of the keyboard smell like dust and scorched electronics. "The Tower Music in Boston has a whole floor of outsider music. I spent $863 on tapes the last time I was there. Lots of John Zorn. Crazy horns and no tempo." I don't think the term "harsh noise" had been coined yet at that point in history, but he's describing it perfectly.

The electronics fire stench is overpowering, so I move to the hallway outside the room, playing a game on a Mac Plus compact computer. The entire floor of the common area is covered in neoprene mousepad material, and smells heavily of synthetic fumes, like a spermicidal condom. The game is like *Breakout*, but involves people throwing fetuses out of building windows, and you have to bat them back in the air with a coat hanger, similar to my peanut butter stirrer.

After twenty minutes, a long-haired guy runs out of his room and starts screaming and pointing his finger at me, yelling at me not to play blasphemous games at a state university. He's more of a jock-o long-hair, like a guy who was serious about ultimate frisbee. I yank the power cord out of the wall, grab the computer by the carry handle on top, and walk to the library to hide in the stacks and use their power outlets.

Hours later, when I return to the dorm for more peanut butter, everyone is on the front deck, lighting candles. I ask an albino grunge dude with an afro what happened, and he says the long-haired guy climbed to the top of the center building and jumped, breaking his neck. I ask if anyone knew why he did it, and someone else said he was wanted by the cops for a triple homicide, from a drug deal that went bad years ago, and I feel relieved it wasn't my fault, but also scared that he could have easily killed me, too.

\* \* \*

I think I'm having a heart attack, and there are no hospitals in town anymore, because they were all Blockbuster-branded trauma centers and went out of business. I go to a Pep Boys car store, because I heard they let you use their diagnostic equipment for free. I'm hoping they had an ultrasound machine, or the EEG things you hook up to your chest to measure heart waves.

A cooler sits in front of the store, filled with free samples of a new Mountain Dew flavor that is purple. The label says "BRUTAL PURPLE!" and has lightning bolts on it. I chug one, and the heart attack sensation goes away, but it tastes horrible, and the aftertaste is even worse.

I buy two more cans of the soda, plus a jumbo-size of Corn Nuts, and talk to a guy with no teeth who is putting a big-block semi engine into a Chevette. He's missing six fingers, but says he can still play guitar with a spatula, as long as he uses an open tuning.

\* \* \*

Somewhere in a mountain town... it looks like the city from *Red Dawn*, a single main drag of two-story brick buildings, big sky overhead... I'm riding a BMX bike with tiny wheels and no gears, looking for an address that isn't there. 414 South Mitchell — it's written on the back of my hand, supposed to be the location of a witch doctor, but I'm rolling past tiny craftsman homes on postage stamp lots, and that particular number is missing. 410, 412, 416, 418. I back up, look again, no 414.

The back tire pops — ran over a nail — and I push the bike to a party store, a place that sells streamers and balloons. I figure they have helium tanks, and I've got a pack of Big Red gum. I could chew myself a patch, then fill the tire with laughing gas, maybe huff a few toots for the road. The clerk is this beautiful college-aged woman who looks like a Czech swimsuit model from the Eighties, and she's watching *The Empire Strikes Back* on a little TV behind the counter. She tells me helium made her sister bipolar, so they only use carbon monoxide at the store.

I abandon the bike, chain it to the back of a copy shop... I'm in the basement of a Chinese grocery, looking at bags of rice, metal gasoline cans of soy sauce, none of them with any English on them. A guy behind the counter asks if I want to buy a mainframe computer. Before I can answer, he pulls aside a curtain, revealing a dusty old Amdahl 470, the size of a large refrigerator. It has property tags from Lawrence Livermore National Laboratories on it, and all the power and data cables have been cut with a machete. I quote something from the first Primus album and run.

Outside, it's now dusk, and I'm on the south side of a large college campus, tall limestone buildings opposite a strip of pizza joints and used record stores. I'm walking down an alley, and the graffiti on the back walls of the building is moving, throbbing, grotesque, like a Ralph Steadman illustration come to life. A guy who looks like Alan Parsons wanders the alley, collecting cans from garbage bins, and mumbling the lyrics to the song "Eye in the Sky." I ask him what time the shops on the street closed, and he says something snarky about time being an abstract concept, then asks me for a dollar for weed. I ignore him, keep walking.

I think I spot Geraldo Rivera in the parking lot of a Village Pantry gas station, but it's just a guy who looks like Geraldo Rivera. He's with a camera crew, interviewing the owner of a local pizza joint. The pizza baron's face is burned and deformed, like he went bobbing for french fries in a hot broiler pan full of grease. He says someday, his pizza place will become so large, he will personally bankrupt the NFL and save America from Communism. I yell "FUCK OLIVES! BABA BOOEY!" at the boom mic operator, but I'm sure they will cut it out.

When I go into the Village Pantry to buy some candy bars and a Gatorade, the same woman from the party store is behind the counter, eating day-old fried chicken from the hot bar next to the cash register and talking to the cashier about her bipolar sister. I don't think she recognizes me. When I ask her if the old chicken is discounted, she just looks at me.

* * *

Ten people die of heart attacks during a Krispy Kreme competitive eating contest. It's held in Times Square, and I'm there, because there's only one Bank of America ATM in the entire city, and I have to go to the basement of the Pizza Hut next to the MTV studios to withdraw cash without paying an extra dollar. I'm fighting through the crowd, trying to get to the

Pizza Hut, and I step on a severed human arm, which squishes like an overfilled jelly donut. I keep walking, because if I stop to report it to NYPD, there goes my lunch hour.

Someone from Johnson and Johnson or Unilever or another big soap company is handing out samples of their knockoff Bioré pore strip, and telling people that the Bioré company is owned by the Illuminati and kills babies. It reminds me too much of the "Procter and Gamble is Satanic" trope from the Eighties, but I take some of the strips anyway. They look like they were designed by a baby boomer and marketed towards millennials, and say "Hey, Grunge and Shit!" on them.

Later that evening, I'm eating sushi made out of peanut butter and rice, and have *Requiem for a Dream* on for background noise. I'm examining my nose pores in a hand mirror, and they look like the surface of one of Jupiter's moons. I slap on one of the pore strips, and when the movie gets to the infamous "ass to ass" scene, I rip off the piece of chemical-coated plastic. It's covered with stringy tentacles of pus, some four to six inches long, like entire blood vessels in my nose and face were full of hardened pus. I look in the mirror and every pore is now shooting pulsating streams of blood like a garden soaker hose. I try to take a Polaroid of my face, but the flash doesn't work right, and the picture is just a glowing ball of blue light on a black background.

* * *

Everyone leaves town for some reason. It seems completely normal, like people only live here for 50 weeks out of the year, then drop everything and flee for two weeks in the summer. It feels like when college campuses are completely vacant the week after finals, but this is a town of maybe 50,000 people with no university. It has a slight atomic apocalypse vibe, but it's a nice spring day outside, no nuclear winter.

I have a small Citroen car that's not much more than a motorcycle with seats and doors, but I'm too busy trying to repair a boat in my garage to drive it. I have a girlfriend, or an ex-girlfriend maybe (depending on who you asked) who lives in Tampa, and I want to drive cross-country to see her, but I'm not sure the car would make the first hundred miles without exploding. It also runs on a mixture of gasoline and cheese; you have to pack a small tank under the hood with a Reblochon or something similar, and it's really hard to find in the Midwest. You can't just go to an IGA in rural Indiana and pick up a runny unpasteurized cheese. (I don't know, maybe the Amish sell it at a roadside stand.)

The girlfriend/ex-girlfriend shows up back in town, and says she flew back in a wooden biplane to sign some paperwork saying I was never in the Army, which she needs for a financial aid thing. I bring her to a new restaurant in the mall. It used to be a McDonald's, but it was converted into an old-school Russian place, covered in aged, rustic wood, like a beat-up Dacha in Siberia, something straight out of a Tolstoy novel.

The servers are all old, decrepit Russian ladies, the total Babushka look, with wrinkled faces, white hair done up in scarves, Slav as hell. The tables are slabs of logs, completely unfinished. The waitress gives us menus that are single xeroxed sheets, but the first side is filled with listings of real estate, cars, and jewelry for sale. I think it's a joke and say, "I'll have this and this and this" and point at three different houses. Then I realize the breakfast menu was on the back side, and I'd just spent $485,000 on real estate in the Baltics.

* * *

I'm on a computer repair gig at a girl's apartment, working on her IBM PCjr, installing a modem she bought to watch the Indianapolis 500 on CompuServe. None of the slots inside the computer line up correctly with the card, and it's like shoving ten pounds of shit in a five-pound sack. She plugs in the computer while I'm working on it and starts flipping the power switch back and forth, saying, "Does that help?" Smoke pours from the motherboard like a jet engine exploding. But instead of the usual silicon-burning blue soot, it's thick green smoke with the skunky odor of toxic weed. I assume she's going to hold me responsible for replacing the machine, but she apologizes profusely and says it's her fault because she never goes to church anymore.

The girl's roommate comes home as I'm trying to put out the computer fire with a wet handkerchief. The roommate is incredibly attractive, a sort of Nineties version of young Kirstie Alley with long red-brown hair. She thinks I'm just a friend of her roommate, and starts talking loudly about how she's catfishing an East German grad student over the VAX mainframes at school, getting him to send her free food and coupons. She's drinking the juice from a jar of pickles as she talks.

My customer tells the roommate that I'm the computer guy, and she immediately lights up. "Do you want to take A-201 accounting for me? I can give you my car. It's a 1988 Chevy S-10 that's been lowered and completely customized. It has an Alpine stereo." I tell her they check IDs on test days now, and the homework is all computerized, so the plan won't work. Also, I don't know anything about accounting; I'm not a business major. I did used to sleep with an accounting professor's girlfriend, but after a few weeks, she went nuts and moved to Syria to work as an assistant manager at a KFC chain there.

We box up the burned-out computer; the plan is to bring it to the Electronics Boutique store in the mall and return it with no receipt, tell the clerk it was the wrong color or something. She's attractive, and has large breasts, so this will probably work. I don't have a car, so she borrows the roommate's slammed truck. It scrapes and groans with every bump and turn. At the mall, I realize I don't remember the girl's name, and I have to eat.

I leave her at the computer store, and go to a Sbarro pizza. They have hired strippers to stand in front of the store and rub slices of pizza on their genitals. Father Guido Sarducci is sitting at a table outside the entrance, eating a slice while smoking a cigarette and watching the ladies. All the slices of pizza in the glass case on the counter have bizarre toppings, like cockroaches and artichoke hearts, so I leave, forget about the computer job, and walk home from the mall, even though it's only nine degrees out and for some reason dark in the middle of the day.

* * *

A guy with the username CowboyBob79 has an insane wife telling everyone on Yahoo Answers that eating avocado pits cures leukemia and cystic fibrosis. When people complain about losing teeth she just says, "TRY HARDER" and posts horribly mangled Forrest Gump inspirational quotes. I'm reading the posts on a Palm Pilot while I'm waiting for a bus to my harp lesson. My first instinct is to check if all of my teeth are intact, because I've been having a long run of dental trauma nightmares, like the recurring dream where I'm riding on the back of a Harley and fall off face-first and scrape my incisors down to stumps on the rough asphalt.

I bought a harp online for some reason, I don't know why. I drag it on the bus to daily lessons with a 117-year-old woman who claims she played electric trombone on the *Wizard of Oz* soundtrack. I want to learn some heavy metal songs, like old Metallica or Black Sabbath, but she spends the first ten lessons teaching me how to tune the harp and play the major scale. She's almost entirely deaf, and instead of an electronic hearing aid, she holds this thing up to her ear that looks like a viking horn and yells at me to talk louder.

I give up on music and trade the harp for an old car made by the Robotron computer corporation in East Germany. It has a three-and-a-half cylinder engine and no steering wheel, just a pair of levers you push and pull, like the controls on a tank. I bring the car to an Olive Garden filling station, where they give me unlimited breadsticks as they flush the car's crankcase with marinara sauce and garlic-infused olive oil. The waiting room has a French version of the *Asteroids* video game, but I put in a quarter, and none of the controls work.

A nervous-looking guy with a bulbous nose comes to the register and starts screaming at the cashier. "I've got a gluten allergy and this wallpaper was put up with wheat paste! I'm going to sue you; I'm going to sue the Olive Garden corporation; I'm going to sue the builder; I'm going to sue the wallpaper manufacturer; I'm going to sue the illegal aliens who hung the wallpaper; I'm going to sue the government, state local federal, whoever. I'm even suing the government of Italy, even though this shit isn't real Italian food." (Who goes to Olive Garden if they have a gluten allergy, anyway?)

I check on my car, and it's sixteen feet in the air on a hydraulic lift, with the engine on the ground in pieces. Two mechanics are listening to an Easy-E free jazz album and playing Russian roulette with a gold-plated revolver. I show up just in time for one of them to blow his head off.

\* \* \*

I'm at a mall where every store is a Wetzel's Pretzel. They are not all pretzel stands, though; there are Wetzel's Pretzel shoe stores, pretzel jewelry shops, sit-down pretzel restaurants, and a few pretzel-themed department stores, three-story anchor buildings with men's pretzels, women's pretzels, intimate pretzels, and so on. It's a double-decker shopping center, and it takes me about four hours to walk the perimeter of a single floor.

Earlier, it was hailing and thundering like a biblical story outside, and I thought for sure the skylights in the mall would get blown out. But the storm passed as suddenly as it started, so I walk to the out-buildings across from the mall. Every car in the parking lot has extensive damage from the storm, most probably totaled, and a symphony of car alarms are still going off in a chain reaction. Across the way, I find a Chinese seafood restaurant that has nothing to do with pretzels, and go inside. It smells like when you are a kid and you put a bucket of seashells in your mom's car trunk, then don't remember to take them out for a month. I duck out and go next door, to a Qdoba taco place.

The only employee working the register is Taylor Swift. She's trying to play an acoustic guitar and write a song about an ex-boyfriend while she works the cash till. Her guitar, an expensive pre-war Martin, is covered in taco sauce and fajita grease. I think this scenario would be a great idea for a concept album, where she's playing part of a song about a guy who betrayed her, and then after thirty seconds, she yells, "Can I get those three Mad Rancher tacos with a side of queso?" It might resonate with millennials who are all stuck in dead-end jobs, I don't know.

I order a burrito salad and fill a baseball cap with nacho cheese for the road. A pimply teen-ager brings out my tray of food, and it comes with a three-foot machete. It's unclear if I'm supposed to return the blade when I'm done eating, or if it's a free promotional thing. It's a nice knife, with a sharp edge and blued steel. It even has a hollowed-out handle filled with emergency supplies, like those old Rambo knives back in the day. I ask the kid behind the counter if the knife is free, and he rolls his eyes and says, "NO HABLA."

\* \* \*

I take the bus to a gymnasium in Fort Lee, New Jersey where they're holding Olympic auditions. I heard they were adding chain-link fencing as an event, and thought I could qualify, since I used to sell fencing at Montgomery Wards a decade before.

They have unlimited chicken nuggets at the hospitality table in front of the high school gym, but no sauces or drinks. I eat ten or twelve nuggets anyway, and quickly realize the secret to bulk eating them is you really need both a sauce and a drink. I have a packet of ketchup in my backpack, but eating nuggets with ketchup is disgusting and should be illegal.

I try to talk to the judges inside, but they're all busy filling baby food jars with human teeth that are sitting in a pile on the floor. They make me sign a Hallmark card addressed to the guy who details Toby Keith's truck — he has apparently suffered from an aneurysm and can't operate a vacuum cleaner for two weeks. I look at the card and Tico Torres, the drummer from Bon Jovi, has told the guy Santa Claus is really an IRS agent working under a false name.

* * *

Someone at school told me that Charles Manson wrote five episodes of *Cheers* in 1986 but was not given screen credit due to a WGA arbitration dispute, so I'm watching all eleven seasons on LaserDisc in a small study carrel in the main library. The library has a pro archival LaserDisc player that enables me to watch the episodes at 1.5 times normal speed with crystal-clear clarity. I'm chugging glass bottles of Mountain Dew in the little wood cubicle and have been awake for three or four days, but still haven't found any evidence of Uncle Chuck's writing style.

I give up after about five seasons, and walk to a Big Lots store, where they are still selling Surge soda. I spot the ex-girlfriend of my old friend Andre from high school. She is stocking up on discontinued spermicidal jelly and off-brand Fritos, and has a crazed, vacant look on her face from the perfect mix of meth addiction and religious indoctrination. I watch her shoplift four sticks of butter and eat them whole, without chewing, just deep-throating them one after another. I decide I don't really need the Surge soda and walk home.

* * *

I'm hiking across town to see Monte and his brother Scotty, who have apparently found some Civil War swords buried in a city park, and are trying to use a mixture of orange juice and vinegar to remove the thick layer of rust on the blades. I have a Black and Decker battery-powered angle grinder and I thought we'd try that to clean the metal a bit. It's in my backpack, along with a GG Allin video tape. Monte doesn't even have a TV, let alone a VHS player, but I want to show it to him anyway. He's a bit of a shit-throwing enthusiast, so anything GG-related is welcome there.

On the way, I stop at a hamburger stand which is all old-fashioned with chrome and white tile and neon signs, but it is named FUCKERS. It think maybe I'm reading the cursive writing wrong, or the font was off, but the woman working there says, "WELCOME TO FUCKERS! WOULD YOU LIKE TO TRY OUR DOUBLE FUCKERS?" and I wonder if I'm still somehow hearing her wrong, or how this ever got past people in a place where Damn Yankees had to cancel an appearance at the county fair because people protested a band with a swear word in their name.

It reminds me of a time when I was twelve or thirteen, when I kept seeing a TV commercial for a movie-of-the-week where women were walking around with no shirts on, but their breasts did not have nipples. The ad came up a few times an hour, and each time, I carefully scrutinized the bouncing, nipple-less breasts, and wondered if a law had been passed saying nipples couldn't be shown, but as long as they were missing, the rest of the tit was fine, so the networks started using makeup and effects to conceal the outlaw areolae. It wasn't until I saw the commercial at my friend's house that I realized the truth: the color settings on my old Magnavox TV were completely blown out, and the woman's shirt was a light green, which looked like a flesh-colored hue on the dying cathode ray tube of my set.

When I get to Monte's place, his brother Scotty answers the door, and his right hand is missing, replaced with a really bad fake rubber arm, like the one that guy in *The Fugitive* had. Inside, Monte is lifting a set of weights made from a half-dozen plastic milk jugs filled with urine and tied to a broomstick, like a setup someone would use in prison. He tells me he's up to fifty chin-ups in a row, and if he can get to a hundred, he's joining the Marines and becoming a professional military stock car driver. I try telling him the Marines only sponsor a NASCAR team and don't actually drive the cars, but he starts yelling lines from *Full Metal Jacket* while doing military presses. I know it's only a matter of time before one of the piss jugs knocks into a wall and sprays uric acid everywhere, so I leave.

It's now snowing outside, even though it's July, so I go back to the Fuckers and order a plastic bucket filled with onion rings and nacho cheese, which is their themed dish. The waitress, who looks like Pam Dawber, tells me if I can eat 80 of them without going to the bathroom, they will give me a job making a dime above minimum wage.

* * *

I'm skateboarding in a mall fountain (I do not know how to skateboard in real life — I'm lucky I can walk on most days). My friend Gary is explaining to me how the Mattel *Dungeons and Dragons* handheld game released in 1981 is essentially the game *Hunt the Wumpus* with the icons changed, and it completely sucks. I haven't seen it yet — my parents just bought me the Sears ripoff version of the *Simon* game with the four LED lights you hit in various combinations until you get fed up with it and throw it into a wall. It takes 16 D-cell batteries, which power it for about ten minutes, tops. The bootleg version also only has one color light. Actually, I think they may have just bought me a lantern and said it was a video game.

We take all the coins out of the fountain and buy a Spyro Gyra album on 8-Track, and blast it in the parking lot for an hour. (Gary's Camaro has an aftermarket 8-Track tape deck that's mounted in the glove compartment, and sounds like total shit.) Later, we decide to take all the wiring out of Gary's car and lay it end-to-end to see if it will stretch across the entire equator. I guess he read this fact in *Dear Abby* or something. The wiring harness ends up being only about sixty feet long, and we never get his car started again.

\* \* \*

The Oakland Greyhound station has a time-space portal that leads to Bloomington, Indiana in 1992, shortly before the IU basketball team lost the Final Four game to Duke, 78-81. The portal, sitting next to a newspaper stand, looks like that hatch from *Lost*, covered in layers and layers of institutional gray paint. A security keypad resembling a Radio Shack calculator is glued to the hatch, with the rubbery six key completely worn down, but the others numbers glossy and new. I enter 6666 and the hatch opens. A long poured concrete hallway that reminds me of the movie *THX-1138* leads to another door, same keypad, same combination.

When I walk through the portal, I'm in the basement of the Indiana Memorial Union on April 4, 1992. There's a freak snowstorm outside, blanketing the city in white. I know I totaled my car that day, broke the passenger door off when it popped open and hit an ice drift, although I don't know if this is on an alternate timeline. (It resulted in only like a hundred dollars of damage, but the car was worth less than that. I drove it without a door for the next six months and then abandoned it at a monster truck rally.) I walk to the crash site to watch the wreck happen, and I'm amazed and depressed at how thin I look back then. I think about placing some sports bets, but the only team I know anything about is the Colorado Rockies, and they won't exist for another year.

After watching the car accident, I trudge to a buffalo wings place and ask them to sell me every wing in the store, since they were five cents each. (I'm not sure how I paid — no Apple Pay, no credit cards or money from 1992, and any currency would have been bills from decades in the future.) I eat the wings and wonder if there is some sickness I could get from not having immunity to certain enzymes or amino acids that had mutated over the last 25 years, like how vegetarians who eat meat get violently ill.

I can't find the return portal, and half-realize I am in a dream, so I try to force my brain to change the scenery to lead back to current day. (Sometimes this works. I remember having a dream once about wandering around the strip of fast food restaurants outside a mall, and forcing a Burger King to change into a Hot 'n Now hamburger stand, although when I went to order there, the stand was being operated by former leader of Turkmenistan Saparmyrat Nyýazow, and there were no hamburgers; he offered to make me a salami sandwich on white bread, but I declined.)

I can't use the dream power to recreate the portal, but I do open a web browser somehow, and use it to browse MovieFone's list of upcoming 1992 film releases. I still can't believe they had two piece of shit Christoper Columbus movies come out that year. I can't remember if I ever saw either one, but seriously, fuck Christopher Columbus.

\* \* \*

I drive to my friend Oscar's house so we can go to this Olive Garden ripoff called Breadstick Manor and eat unlimited appetizers for a few hours, then catch the new Van Damme movie. On the way up to his apartment, an FBI agent tells me I have to trick Oscar into answering the door so he can serve him with some papers. If I didn't help him, it was obstruction of justice, and I'd lose my Blockbuster Video renting privileges.

I go to Oscar's apartment door, then tell him that a guy from M&M/Mars had to come in the house to give us free candy bars. He gets really excited about it, but is then pissed off when the FBI guy barges in with no candy. "I really wanted a Snickers, man — even a fun-sized." The agent clamps a thing on Oscar's ankle like a court-mandated alcohol monitoring bracelet, but it plays a hologram like the one Princess Leia hid in R2-D2. The hologram shows Hal Linden from *Barney Miller*, saying, "Only you can prevent forest fires" over and over. The FBI agent says, "I had to wear a diaper for Lent," and then jumps out of the third-story window.

* * *

I'm sleeping in a closet of a friend's house because I have two weeks between apartment leases and nowhere else to stay. I'm working a temp job as an assistant for the president of a minor-league soccer team, mostly answering questions about Lotus 1-2-3. Every morning, I wake up in the mildewy closet, listen to an entire Frank Zappa album while I'm eating Brock's pick-a-mix candy for breakfast, then shower in an old claw foot tub that's rigged into a shower with a rubber hose and plastic curtain hung from the ceiling. After bathing, I walk to work, which takes about an hour.

I drive a desk in the basement of a cinderblock building once filled with offices of nuclear weapons designers, and spend every day waiting for phone calls and stupid questions. The soccer team works out of a set of cubicles nearby, mostly jerking off to videotapes of Pelé playing on a big-screen TV in the break room. The upstairs floors are occupied by engineers performing an FAA study that involves throwing cadavers into jet engines, digitizing the data, and producing a report nobody will ever read. They don't actually put the dead bodies into the engines on site; that's all done in Mexico, to get around some law about desecrating corpses. They mostly do SAS/SPSS data analysis here.

The job pays me in NYC MTA subway slugs. I don't think you can use them anymore, except maybe to make nostalgic cufflinks to sell on Etsy. I'm talking to a guy upstairs with an outdated haircut from the Eighties, trying to get him to buy some tokens, like as a memorabilia piece. I've got a gallon-size ziploc bag full of the slugs, and I haven't moved a single one yet. He tells me I should go to a Subway restaurant and see if they'll take them.

\* \* \*

I go to an AAMCO transmission shop because the skin on my hands is exfoliating in sheets, falling off in big chunks. I can't visit a doctor for some reason, a fear of getting caught or put in the system maybe, so I go to the transmission place because they advertise a lot on the radio. ("Double A *honk honk* M-C-O") The guy at the shop tells me he can't get me in for an appointment for six months, and in the meantime, I should wear a special set of loofah gloves, and avoid malls and full-serve restaurants. I ask him if he can take a quick look if I give him an extra twenty bucks, and he offers to give me a ride to a Subway sandwich shop above a ballet school out by the highway, where I can tell the cashier to make me onion rings from the secret menu.

This must have been the early 90s, when Subway shops didn't always smell like warm puke and fake bread, way before they hired a fat pedophile as their spokesperson. The menu looks like it was designed with *Star Wars* fonts, and they also serve old-school Chinese food, like chop suey and chow mein. I'm not hungry, and order a wax paper carton filled with Pepsi, and a foam cup of ice. The cashier tells me they had stand-up comedy at four, but I'm not interested. I sit in a booth, chug the Pepsi (which is flat, but all Pepsi tastes flat to me) and read a newspaper, which has an entire section devoted to real estate closings and arson jobs.

Walking to a library after the Pepsi, I notice my hands are better, but I enter the weird dream state where I can't follow linear time, keep thinking about how the Paseo Padre Parkway runs north after you cross the Dumbarton bridge from Palo Alto to the East Bay. It passes several anonymous biotech companies, identical two-story office buildings covered in chrome and mirrored windows, that could be designing weapons of tomorrow, or maybe chewable vitamins. The road eventually leads to a sprawl of townhouse condominiums with no external doors; they were built to add scenery to flight simulator video games that would eventually map the local terrain. It was cheaper to build the fake condos instead of drawing them in the game, because of tax subsidies or something.

That's what the guy at the gas station says, anyway. It's a full-serve only station, because the city is named Newark, and even though this was California, there's a Newark in New Jersey, so that gas-pumping law still applies. I'm driving from Seattle to Mexico with everything I own in the trunk of a subcompact, wanting to buy a microwave burrito or candy bar for second lunch while this guy who looks like a young Richard Pryor overfills my car at like ten bucks a gallon.

"They also built a Jack in the Box hamburgers across the street, part of the same package. Larry David ate there. Well, not *that* one. He ate at *a* Jack in the Box, on his show. You ever see it? Funny as shit." The guy is pumping hundreds of gallons of gas into my Toyota Yaris, while I'm writing in a little Moleskine notebook, trying to jot down everything I knew about Lenny Bruce, for a blog article. (Comedian, obscenity trial, "Masked Man" cartoon, heroin overdose, found dead on a toilet, I think. Didn't care for his stand-up, but I only saw one of the late recordings, where he was just reading court transcripts.)

I walk to the Jack in the Box while the gas all over my car dries. I want to get one of the little ball antenna toppers, but they are out. The zit-encrusted teenager on the register says he'll sell me fifty tacos for five dollars, and I take the deal, but I only get through four before I get sick of tacos for the year.

\* \* \*

The National Guard has been mobilized, allegedly because of Godzilla attacks on Chicago, but there is no Godzilla, and the whole thing is a ploy to fuck people out of insurance benefits, or write more parking tickets. I walk to 7-Eleven to buy a newspaper, and the *Sun-Times* is running a Mike Royko editorial about giant monsters on the front page. I think about buying the whole stack of papers, wrapping them individually in plastic, and selling them ten years from now as collector's items, but then I remember how every flea market has a guy unable to unload JFK assassination or Apollo moon landing newspapers for a dollar each. On the way to the convenience store, I notice a set of new moles on my arms, and when I look them up on a braille translation web site, I find they say, "This is your brain on drugs, LOL."

\* \* \*

A guy at the bus stop is cutting off his fingers with a pair of poultry shears and shouting lyrics from Black Sabbath's "War Pigs." (I can't repeat the lyrics here without getting sued by Sharon Osbourne.) I'm idling next to the bus shelter, driving a Chevy Impala with no top — I cut the roof off with a Jaws of Life at a fire station. The car still has a windshield on it, but it's hanging on like a loose tooth ready to fall out. The whole vehicle flexes and bows when I make even the slightest of turns, and I know it's only a matter of time before the front subframe breaks loose during a high-speed turn and kills me.

I'm stuck in front of the bus stop because it's where two eight-lane roads meet, and the traffic light is red for like twenty minutes. When it turns green, the guy yells "420 BLAZE IT!" at me, while squirting blood everywhere.

I lay down a long burn out, and then drive to a mall parking lot, where a guy in a Yanni t-shirt is changing the oil on both engines of an F-15E Strike Eagle jet, dumping the old fluids on the asphalt with no drain pan. I ask him if he's in the Air Force, because I was born on an Air Force base and I know a lot about the *Ace Combat 4* video game, and he says no, he impulse-bought the jet from Israel in a fit of consumer therapy while whacked out on Ambien. I look at the plane's markings, and instead of flags or stars, it has Xanax bars painted on each wing. In cursive below the cockpit, it says "GLUTEN WARRIOR."

I walk across the parking lots of the mall, worried about where I can cash a paycheck. The asphalt is insanely cracked and worn, the crevices filled with a rubbery black sealing compound. Most of the banks inside the mall have been converted into vape stores or pain-management clinics, and I'm hoping to luck out and find a big chain of a predatory finance company nearby.

My paper check has a memo line where the payroll department always prints various platitudes and stupid quotes. I'm not sure why I still get paper checks — most people I know are paid with direct deposit or Walmart coupons. When I examine this particular bank draft, the dot-matrix memo reads "A LINE HAS TWO SIDES/DIE IN A FIRE/GO RAIDERS/FUCK THE 49ERS."

There's a credit union across from the fabric store, an asymmetric building that looks like a stoned vegan architect in the Seventies designed it on a dare. It's made of white stucco, now nicotine-yellow and covered in brown water stains from years of deferred maintenance. I expect it to be air conditioned to an excessive degree like most financial institutions, but it's actually heated and humid inside, like a sauna or the tropical rainforest room in a botanical garden. My glasses fog up instantly, and I stumble to the front desk.

The teller is a girl who went to my high school. I didn't know her, but she was in my biology class when we dissected fetal pigs, and she brought in her own butcher tools, all with pink handles. I'm sure she doesn't recognize me — I weigh about double what I did as a teenager, not that it's that hard, since I had the physique of Christian Bale in *The Machinist* back then. She cashes the check — something like $225, and gives me all one dollar bills. I shove the fat stack of money in my wallet, which now looks like a George Costanza billfold. Back in my car, I sit at a 45-degree angle from the thickness of the money in my back right pocket, and think I might end up driving in left-hand circles if I don't take out my wallet, but I'm too lazy to do anything about it.

While I'm driving home, one of the front wheels pops off and rolls away, like how the hubcaps come off every time the General Lee sticks a jump in *The Dukes of Hazzard*. I stop and can't find the tire — it kept rolling, and went straight into a marsh, sank to the bottom. Someone will probably find it in fifty years and wonder what kind of asshole threw a perfectly good tire into a swamp. Oddly, the car still drives and handles fine for the rest of the trip. Maybe it was balanced by the fat wallet. When I get home, I look under the wheel well and find the ball joints and tie rods of the car are missing, replaced with duct tape and pages ripped from a *Thomas the Tank Engine* book.

\* \* \*

I'm in the Navy, serving on a ship called the USS Gravy. It's a gravy tanker, a million-gallon, Exxon Valdez-size oil barge but it carries gravy, soup, and bouillon to combat zones. The US military runs on meat juice, so it's a vital mission. My living quarters on the ship are a small metal state room with a foam cot and an Atari 2600 that can only play the *Air-Sea Battle* cartridge.

We're steaming at full power toward Djibouti, because of a plague or famine or something, carrying sixty-two million gallons of ham and beans around the Horn of Africa. Some pirates try to board off the coast of Somalia, but they're vegans or Muslims or something, because once they find out about our cargo, they apologize and leave at full speed.

I play tuba in the service, and spend most of the long trip learning jazz standards on the brass instrument. Right before we reach the location of our humanitarian mission, an Iraqi jet fires an Exocet anti-ship missile at us and I somehow lose my tuba in the confusion. The rest of the dream is a lengthy court-martial trial with lots of paperwork involving exactly what kind of tuba I had and what tuning it used.

* * *

It looks like the hotel from *Lost in Translation*, but I'm in Berlin, not Japan. I'm somewhere near Potsdamer Platz, where it's all built up with brand new glass buildings and tourist attractions. I remember a picture an old buddy sent me of the same area during the Cold War, all barren concrete and bomb craters, barbed wire fences and The Wall. Now, it's the Blue Man Group and the Sony Center, and the view out of my floor-to-ceiling window is spectacular.

For some reason, Greg Ginn from Black Flag is recording an *Access: Hollywood* episode in my bathroom, doing an interview with one of those interchangeable video host babes. He's talking about how an important part of making it as a punk rock musician is to buy a good condo at a low interest rate, and then list it on Airbnb when you're on tour. While he talks, he eats a loaf of garlic bread that has currywurst on it, which is a trending meme that week.

I walk to the U-Bahn and get on a train car where every person inside looks like The Edge from U2, wearing beanie skull caps and sunglasses and sporting goatees. I put on my walkman, and listen to a Abe Vigoda spoken word album, where's he's talking about going to a Credence Clearwater Revival show back in the Seventies at the Oakland Coliseum and eating too many pot brownies and twirling around in circles until he passed out. It's a 90-minute cassette tape, but seems to go on for hours.

I get out of the train after the tape ends. I'm in a mall in Pennsylvania that I swear is a *Call of Duty: Modern Warfare 3* level. I walk up and down the various concourses and know exactly where to camp with a sniper rifle and take out people at the spawn point outside the big department store that looks like a Carson's, but had some fictional name, like Cantwell's or Corman's. In the food court, I find an old bakery that's now selling only buckets of gravy, which people are eating with their hands.

I don't want any gravy, but I'm starving. I go to the cash register, and see Daniel Ellsberg (leaker of the Pentagon Papers) working there, slopping gravy into cardboard buckets and smiling nervously. "Heh, m, I have a paradox," he tells me. "I have a paradox. You want any gravy? I have a paradox." I buy a bucket just to be nice, but it smells like rancid cottage cheese, so I throw it in a fountain in the center of the mall and made a wish.

Outside, I steal a newspaper from a machine and it says that Greg Ginn has been killed by a disgruntled Airbnb customer who got upset his condo was not gluten-free. The newspaper has a comment section that's filled with virtue signalers upset at Ginn because he would allow wheat in his house. I wonder if that interview from my hotel bathroom will ever be aired, and if I'd somehow be in the background of a shot and get implicated in his death.

* * *

A chart in the back of *Low Rider* magazine has pictures of fingers and knuckles and tells which joint shape will predict a future heart attack and which ones mean a long life or sexual prowess or whatever else. I'm staring at the chart, then studying my fingers, and my digits look like none of the pictures on the chart and I get really worried that I have a rare genetic disease or am secretly half-alien or was adopted from a pack of albino Sasquatch or something. I want to look it up in an online medical site, but I know I'll end up thinking I have prostate cancer within an hour.

\* \* \*

A guy who looks like Iggy Pop with an afro is handing out samples of a Dorito's-flavored lube in front of the Trader Joe's, squirting dollops into people's bare hands. I'm going to the grocery store to buy a new car battery and a plate of sushi, but get distracted by a Pizza Hut down the street that's on fire. The flames smell exactly like the magic dust they spread on top of the breadsticks, and people are licking the soot and debris off the sidewalk.

Inside the grocery store, a slow jam from a hair metal band of the early Nineties blasts through the intercom — Winger, maybe, or Whitesnake. Actually Paul Gilbert, the guitar player from Mr. Big, is working one of the front registers, wearing an old-school pair of over-the-ear headphones, the kind that look like the hearing protectors baggage handlers on a tarmac might use. I nod hello as I stroll in, then realize I didn't know if my car takes a standard 12-volt battery, or if it uses some metric European nonsense, like a 20-millijoule-per-hectare battery.

A group of four men in military uniforms fold a flag from on top of a coffin in the middle of aisle seven, then up-end the casket and dump a body wrapped in aluminum foil into a frozen food chest, next to the egg rolls. An old lady with a cane turns to me and said, "It's like what they did to Ted Williams after he got killed in Viet Nam. Freeze his noggin and thaw it out when they invent the cure. Live forever." One of the soldiers hands the woman the flag, and I notice it wasn't a US flag, but some *Star Trek* thing, like the Klingon flag or Tatooine flag or something.

The Trader Joe's continues on a downward slope endlessly into the ground, like a secret government warehouse carved into a salt flat to store nuclear waste and UFO parts. Every 100 yards, a cardboard cutout of Cindy Crawford holds up a rectangular sign that says "internal organs!" or "post-apocalypse government continuity currency!" I want to ask someone where I can find the car batteries, or maybe something to drink, but all the employees have been replaced by robots, and I think I was supposed to download an app to talk to them, but I lost cell signal miles ago.

Somewhere around the diesel engine section, I find a set of knotted ropes that lead through a narrow concrete tube, back to the surface. I clearly remember not being able to climb the rope in gym class when I was a freshman in high school and we had that Ronald Reagan fitness test. I think aside from lack of upper body strength, I also had an extreme fear of sliding down the hemp rope and permanently burning my thighs on the thick fibers. There was also a rumor in my class that someone caught AIDS on the rope. But this time, I have no trouble climbing, even though I weigh twice as much.

After an hour of rope traversal, I find a thick hatch like a submarine, unscrew it, and emerge in the middle of a snow-covered field in Provo, Utah. A construction crew is using a front-loader to stack giant piles of cash, to burn in a bonfire and summon the ghost of Jesus.

\* \* \*

I'm riding a longboard painted with various Danzig logos, carrying a set of crystal glassware and trying not to break anything. This is in Indiana, and I have to cruise on the shoulder of US-33, because the sidewalks are all uneven, cracked, and covered with broken glass and car parts. I'm supposed to meet a doctor who is selling a Toyota robot that can weld and play chess, but he can't leave his house, because he fell off a roof in a Freemason commune and broke his spine in four places. I probably won't buy the robot, and I definitely can't bring it home on a skateboard, but I do want to check it out. But when I get to his trailer, he's in the middle of selling his pain pills to a cop, and I don't want to get arrested as an accessory or accomplice or anything, so I leave.

I go to a two-screen movie theater next to a strip mall, and both screens are playing *Silence of the Lambs*, but one is dubbed in German. The concession stand doesn't have any Junior Mints or Twizzlers, just tacos made with spam and a knock-off Christian Halloween candy with bible phrases on the package. I don't technically eat spam and I'm sure the candy tastes like shoe polish, so I just buy an extra-large RC Cola and drag it to the English theater.

The movie seems to be running at half-speed, and right as I start thinking about how young Jodi Foster looked back in 1991, the film skips off the spindles, gets jammed, and melts in the projector. There are only a half-dozen people in the auditorium, and everyone but me is asleep. Someone in the front row wakes up from their nap and throws a large beverage at the screen. The soda runs down the mixed-fiber fabric of the silver screen, creating a strange, shimmering pattern, like a hippy light show at a psychedelic band concert. A projectionist turns on the house lights, leans out of the little window by the ceiling, and says go home, the film is over. He throws packs of cigarettes to each person, and says we can go to the German version next door for half price.

I'm not paying twice to read subtitles. I go back outside and watch a street vendor grinding out sausages and hamburger meats from a Hobart machine on a trailer behind a Ford Escort. I offer the guy the Marlboros I got from the projectionist and ask him how much meat he'd give me for them. He looks at the cigarette package, which has giant letters on the side that said "WILL KILL YOU" and then hands it back, says all his meat is freezer-burned and tastes horrible. "It's good to feed to dogs, if you have one you hate."

Someone wheels a Conrail box car across the parking lot on a spur line half-buried in the asphalt. They push the car with an orange pickup truck which has outrigger wheels on it so it could work on roads or rails. When it stops, the door opens, and a bunch of guys dressed like Jack Kerouac jump out, start playing bongos and reading free-association slam poetry. "Groovy! Groovy! Blow, baby! Blow!"

* * *

At a redneck computer store, between a laundromat and a dialysis center in a strip mall — a guy with a mullet and spiked hair on top has a name tag that says "Skeeter" on it. He beats a beige tower computer with a ball peen hammer. Smoke is pouring out of the machine, and it reminds me of a competitive vaping show I saw on ESPN once. Skeeter tells me the customer should have stuck with the 386. (This is years after the Pentium had come out.)

I ask for some sticks of RAM for my Macintosh, and he smirks, points to a well-worn *Computer Shopper* magazine on the counter and tells me to pick out what I want, add 20%, and he'd order it for me. I was going to state the obvious, that I could just order it myself, but he starts up the hammering again and can't hear me.

There's a Chi-Chi's Mexican restaurant across the street, and I think about telling them it's my birthday to get the fried ice cream. But then I remember their hepatitis outbreak that killed a bunch of people, and go to Steak and Shake instead, where I'll definitely get food poisoning, but not hep-C.

* * *

On the walk down the steep hill to Pioneer Square... I think I see the arcade from the movie *Tron*, and have a sudden vision of entering a video game forever, turning my soul into pixelated images. It makes me wonder if any thoughts, feelings, or emotions beyond those generated in the game would be trapped within me, or if they would vanish, like a high-resolution image converted to 640x480 in Microsoft Paint, all fine details vanishing forever in the downsampling.

The Ivar's fish shop on the waterfront smells like rotting clams, but I go in anyway, to get some french fries and drench them in enough malt liquor sauce to embalm myself. Inside, I see my girlfriend from my freshman year of college, working the drive-through window. (The restaurant is on the water, but still has a drive-through window, probably because all locations were built from the same floor plan. They use the window to serve to small boats and people on jet skis or in canoes and kayaks.) I can't let her spot me — I told her back in 1990 that I needed an emergency liver transplant and had to move to Yugoslavia — so I carefully slip back out of the store.

I find a book shop that specializes in UFO maps written in German. The owner looks exactly like a young Peter Gabriel, wearing white face makeup with various black scribbles and outlines painted on it. He plays an out-of-tune flute and talks to a picture of a dolphin on the wall, a sort of aquatic mammal altar, with candles and incense sticks burning on a shelf beneath it. I ask him if he had any books on *Star Wars* and he looks at me like I'm insane, so I leave.

A man on roller skates playing Primus songs on a bass guitar comes up to me on the street and asks if I want to buy any candy bars for Jesus. I look down at my hands, and they are bleeding — the stigmata. I wave around the bloody appendages and tell the guy maybe he should give me his candy bar money. He skates away, and I walk home, wondering if I need to get a tetanus shot or put any Neosporin on my miraculous nail wounds.

\* \* \*

I'm painting the side of a three-story brick building in a Midwestern small town, using a Wagner power sprayer, but instead of a cup of latex paint, it's hooked up to an institutional-size glass bottle of Aunt Jemima's syrup. My shoulder is covered in stick-on electrodes that are plugged into a cheap Chinese electronic pain massager thing. It's causing my arm to jerk and spasm with the therapeutic pulses of energy, spraying the syrup in every direction. The building's champagne brick is covered in decades of black soot. The odor of diesel particulate matter and maple syrup fills the air, and it's honestly not that bad.

A guy comes up to me carrying a ventriloquist dummy that looks like it's been run over by a car and left in the rain for a year. He tells me he's the BTK killer, and I ask him if that name is redundant, since it stands for "Bind, Torture, Kill Killer" which is like an ATM machine or CMS system. He gets pissed off and tells me I'm going to hell for using an air compressor. I consider going to Sears to buy a second air compressor, just to seal the deal, but the nearest Sears that hasn't been shut down is something like 45 hours away.

After finishing the wall, I go to a restaurant downtown that only serves two things: Salisbury steak or fried ice cream. I order the ice cream, and sit down at the only seat, a two-up table with tall barstools in the front window. A neon sign hanging from the ceiling is flickering on and off. While waiting for my food, I realize it is flashing in morse code, spelling out the letters T-O-R-T-U-R-E. The table has a leg that is a quarter-inch too short, and rocks back and forth every time I breathe. It makes me think of earthquakes, particularly the 1964 quake in Alaska that hit 9.2 on the Richter scale.

The server brings over my ice cream on a cafeteria tray that was clearly stolen from a mental institution thirty years ago. (It has the logo for the Oregon State Hospital on it.) The ice cream has not been fried — it's a solid frozen scoop, covered in a layer of breading. I ask the server what the hell is going on, if their deep fryer is broken, and he gives me a business card and walks away without saying anything. I look at the card and the front side says "GO FUCK YOURSELF" and the back side has the address and phone number of a bathhouse on it.

I skip the check, leave behind the hardened ball of ice cream, and walk to a bar that has a limited menu of Greek food. They do a side dish where they deep-fry chunks of broccoli and cheese. I used to buy these in the freezer section of Fred Myer, until it got banned by the FDA. Inside, the townies are watching NASCAR on a wall of TVs. The feed is interrupted, and Roger Mudd comes on the two dozen screens, telling us that another Space Shuttle has blown up. Everyone boos and starts throwing food at the monitors, until the bartender pulls out a pump shotgun, chambers two shells, and tells everyone to pay their checks and get the fuck out.

* * *

I'm writing a new zine on the back of wallpaper samples I stole from a home improvement store in the back of a Chuck E. Cheese pizza parlor. It's hard to keep a ball-point pen going on the textured paper, but I scribble furiously for hours. Then I realize it's going to cost me like thirty-seven dollars to mail each issue, and that's just for domestic orders, so I might have to limit the run to like five issues.

One of the articles in the zine is about a futuristic superhero who has gout. He fights crime, but then the bad guys always try to get him to drink beer or eat shellfish to exacerbate his condition and stop him from walking. His sidekick sometimes gives him steroid injections in his feet. I have an idea to write more action/adventure stuff, to possibly sell movie rights, but the story starts a big debate in the gout community, and Stan Lee calls me out in a MySpace diatribe that goes viral because Pauly Shore reposts it. I think it could increase book sales, but it doesn't.

* * *

The outside of my house is covered in barnacles, like it had been underwater for years. Keanu Reaves sits on a plastic bucket and carefully scrapes the walls with a butter knife, trying to remove the crustaceans, with little success. The rhythmic scraping sounds like an East German industrial band minus the lead synth sounds. I vaguely remember offering to pay him a dollar an hour to clean the house, thinking there was some shortcut trick, like spraying the walls in bleach first, so the things fell off. Maybe that's for ticks. Or is that holding them under a cigarette lighter?

A neighbor is on his lawn, using a Jetsons-looking machine to vape tequila. The device has a large glass enclosure, hooked up with wires and tubes to a pump like an air conditioner or power transformer. He sucks the smoky vapor from the transparent chamber with a glass tube, like he's freebasing cocaine. "Tequila is a stimulant. It's a region of Mexico, really," he says. Ten anti-immigration signs and billboards on his front yard, "BUILD THE WALL" galore, and this idiot is addicted to a controlled substance only made in Mexico.

I drive a '76 Nova to the grocery store for taco meat, and while sitting at an intersection behind an Oscar Mayer Wienermobile, I find a secret toggle switch under the dashboard that unveils a set of jump jets and swing wings, for vertical takeoff and short-range flight. I try to fire up the system, but it won't work on regular unleaded gas — a warning light shaped like a dollar sign blinks on the dashboard, indicating I need to fill the tank with premium.

The Kroger is in a strip mall with a rock climbing gym, which used to be a department store, maybe a Lazarus or L.S. Ayres. They gutted the interior and carved in a two-story mountain like the one in *Close Encounters*, using ready-mix concrete and chunks of paving stones. I consider going there, renting a helmet and a pair of crampons, learning to climb the indoor ice wall they created with an old Dairy Queen flash freezer. But I can't do a single pull-up, and the place requires a 250 dollar deposit to rent a ten-dollar helmet, so I don't bother.

On the way into Kroger, I see a guy from my high school who we called Murphy for some reason, even though his real name was Drew Smith. I wave hello — he is leaving the climbing place, and has a thousand feet of rope wrapped over his shoulder, like a bandolier. I ask him what's new, and he says he lost his life savings betting on Notre Dame men's basketball, and the only thing that makes him feel good is climbing until he sweats blood, then kicking himself with his spiked shoes. I nod in agreement, even though I think the whole exercise/endorphins thing was bullshit. He shakes my hand, then walks to his blue Ford Maverick, to load the trunk full of rope and hope his gas tank will not explode.

\* \* \*

I'm wandering through Amsterdam in the rain, carrying a ridiculously large computer tablet that's maybe four feet across, like the size of a piece of framed artwork you'd hang above a fireplace. I'm searching for a Burmese restaurant that's serving Christmas dinner, but it's December 23rd, so everything is booked, filled with corporate holiday parties, drunken businessmen.

I recently started quitting caffeine, because the government banned Coke Zero. I'm trying to ration out my last two cases for as long as possible, drinking a half-can per morning, just to keep myself alive. It isn't working. I'm coughing up a mixture of black mucous and blood, and wondering if I should be alarmed. My health insurance is a negative-100% plan, so any time I go to a doctor, I have to pay double the standard rate. Also, pretty much every nurse I ever see at his practice is wearing *Minions* scrubs, so it's best if I never go to the hospital for anything.

It's misting rain, a constant, cold haze in the darkness. Standing at a large bus platform, a roof with no walls where travelers loiter and buy magazines and heroin, I'm talking to an older Chinese guy, short with no neck, bald on top with the "power donut" hairdo. I know him from somewhere, maybe an old finance gig I had in New York before I freaked out and quit with no notice on a Tuesday. He's explaining to me that the new caffeine laws are going to bankrupt airlines, and I nod and agree like I know what he's talking about. I don't.

\* \* \*

Everyone at the county fair is wearing Japanese face masks and eating french toast on a stick. They all speak a synthesized language, like the background characters in a video game. I didn't know if the masks were a new skin remedy treatment or if they were part of a promotional day, like a new sport-utility vehicle by Nissan; I didn't check the "attire" page for the festival before I arrived. I definitely did not want to stop anyone and ask for an explanation. That's how lawsuits happen.

I have an overwhelming craving for tater tots, an uncontrollable urge for double-fried potatoes with too much salt. I'm also on an Egyptian pyramid kick — probably listening to Iron Maiden's *Powerslave* album too much — I brought an oversized art book about King Tut to the fair, and think I see Freemasonry symbols everywhere. Every carny has an ever-seeing eye somewhere on their signage. *These people may look stupid, but they control the world*, I think.

I go to the concourse with all the freak tents, the booths of bearded women and earless geeks. I find a French-Canadian guy in a cubicle who will explain the metric system for a dollar or three red tickets. Autographs are extra. I pay the entrance fee to see if maybe he wants to geek out about Rush, but he has no idea who they are, thinks Geddy Lee is a hockey player or a famous general. I want my money back, but the guy offers me some of his cold french fries from Wendy's. I don't eat them — I hate Wendy's fries, they are too thick and have the wrong fried-to-potato ratio, and I definitely can't deal with cold fries — but I do appreciate the gesture.

* * *

Grace Slick is chugging sauerkraut juice at my buddy's beer bash, and I feel sorry for her, because her International Harvester lost at the tractor pull. I want to talk to her, but I can't deal with famous people, and I'm trying to fix a broken snow cone machine. Some genius put a jar of chunky peanut butter in the shaved ice chamber, and it's like a car that blew up from sugar in the gas tank. I'd go buy another machine, but it was from Sharper Image, and they're gone, gone, gone...

I'm at a mall in Vegas — maybe one of those shopping concourses between the big casinos, not sure if those are considered malls. I spent twenty-four hours on a plane, and my back's got more knots than a three-dollar sheet of plywood. I find a Sharper Image, or maybe it's a Brookstone, and park my ass in a fake leather massage chair. Every knob is set to eleven, and it feels like Floyd Mayweather is punching me in the back ten times a second.

A sales clerk comes up to me, and she looks like a girl I worked with in a dorm cafeteria back in college. I assume she's going to harass me about buying something or leaving, but she's talking to me about how she's attending a school designed to teach amateur baseball and softball players to eat only meat and fix diesel engines. She's very excited about telling me about the program. I think either she's interested in me sexually, or there's a religious angle, and I can't tell which. She rambles on for 45 minutes, but then the chair breaks and I leave before she can rope me into buying a timeshare vacation package.

I've stolen a city bus from Reno and I'm driving it through an Air Force base in Alaska, crashing through drifts of snow and reading Slayer lyrics on the intercom. A dozen people in the back seats are playing euchre, six people in two partnerships, each team arguing in Dutch (I think, maybe German), screaming furiously about each hand. I have this idea that I will read all the lyrics to every Slayer album in order, but the bus runs on a hydrogen fuel cell, and I don't know how long it will last. I'm also sketchy on a lot of lyrics after *South of Heaven* or so.

I park the bus at a Subway sandwich shop at Elmendorf Air Force Base and tell everyone to get out. A juggling troupe in firefighter gear try to get on the bus, but I flip the signs to "out of service" and tell them to hitchhike to France, where their shit might be tolerated. I lock the bus doors and crawl through the snowdrifts to find a Domino's pizza that sells fireworks.

* * *

There is a pending senate vote on a law to ban all sports — something about an NBA riot in Los Angeles that halted the filming of the *Golden Girls* reunion for The Necrophilia Network (TNN). Rob Lowe is on the mic on C-SPAN2, banging his shoe on the podium like Khrushchev, screaming about the use of plastics in Astroturf. His face looks like that of a stroke victim, stretched and warped by surgeries and injections.

I don't have an opinion either way on the sports thing; I just want reruns of *Scooby Doo* to come back on. I have a master theory that all the episodes have secret codes embedded in them, a treasure map that shows where the dead body of Walt Disney is hidden at the Mall of America in Minnesota. I try to torrent the episodes, but HBO somehow spots my computer connected to a file sharing system, and downgrades my network connection so I can only use a text-only version of Internet Explorer 1.0.

The deliberation ends in a closed-room session. They don't ban sports; the only change is that they will add another round to the Major League Baseball post-season, so it will last until December. They continue to pre-empt all programming though, showing recaps of the hearings and babbling on endlessly about the stock market and the fall sweeps week on prime-time TV.

\* \* \*

I'm walking through an underground mall, a mid-90s neon shopping center in full swing on a Friday night. Everyone is wearing stretch-fabric uniforms from *Star Trek: The Next Generation*, and I don't know if it's for a movie shoot, part of a convention, or if it's a new style that I don't know about. I think it looks stupid, but after walking a million feet of mall, I wonder if I should buy one.

A Suncoast video store is selling a tape of the crucifixion of Christ. It's $19.95 and comes with a free box of M&M's. I don't know if it's the actual crucifixion, or they filmed one of those freaky Filipino guys who do this every year on Good Friday. I also don't know if you get to pick plain or peanut M&M's. I look at the box to see if it has any Peter Gabriel stuff in the soundtrack, but ultimately don't buy a copy, because my VCR got stolen after I got food poisoning from a bad pizza and then threw up during an experimental stage production of *My Fair Lady* where all the cast members were replaced with robotic vacuum cleaners.

I walk through the mall into a connected Hyatt hotel. They have a bank of new AT&T pay phones with video screens, like the primitive ones in the original *Total Recall* movie. I really want to use one, but don't know anyone with a video phone I can call. It's also ten dollars a minute. I go to the front desk of the hotel and tell them I lost an IBM ThinkPad. The clerk pulls out a large box full of old, clunky DOS laptops and tells me to take one. I grab a Dell 486 that weighs 28 pounds and runs on wall power or butane lighter fluid. When I turn it on in the parking lot of a Marathon gas station, it sounds like a jet engine starting up, and the cashier calls the BATF to turn me in for illegal explosives.

* * *

I'm in the bar from *The Shining*, the old-school lounge with the undead bartender serving up drinks and the old picture of the country club and all that jazz. I can't remember the details of the movie, just the conspiracy theories, how Kubrick worked on faking the moon landing or was obsessed with Native American Indians or whatever else was in that stupid documentary. Maybe it was something about aliens. All I know is I'm drinking a bottle of rye whiskey. Rye is an odd liquor; popular during the black-and-white film era, and then it went completely away. Now the hipsters have brought it back, even though it tastes like something used to clean printing press equipment.

That old bartender is explaining to me how the finger lakes in upstate New York have a magnetic anomaly that causes jet-ski accidents with higher frequency. I thought jet-skis were made of plastic and fiberglass, but I guess the engines are probably metal. Come to think of it, the engines are turbines or vacuum pumps of some sort, because the last time I rented one in Florida, they were covered in warning labels about how aiming the jet nozzle at the rectum or vagina would cause severe bodily injury. I had to go home and google it, and found plenty of tasty stories of severe anorectal destruction from people falling off the back of a sea-doo at high speed and getting a 300-horsepower enema.

I drink the bottle of rye and end up outside, in full baseball gear, except I'm still wearing a pair of Wrangler jorts. (U-shape for comfort.) I'm somehow batting leadoff in a Major League game being played at a AAA park, under some weird circumstance, like work made me go and forced me to play. It's at an odd location, like North Carolina or Alabama, and the ballpark is about the size of a Little League diamond, almost no lights, but they had a full video crew televising the game.

I'm the first at-bat of the game. It's against an insanely good pitcher like Clayton Kershaw or young Nolan Ryan, someone with a fastball that would shatter my skull like a ripe melon, even with a batting helmet on, which I don't have. On the first pitch, I barely raise my hands and an off-speed junk ball ricochets off the end of the bat and bloops between the pitcher and first. I run like an Alabama judge at a Girl Scout jubilee and manage to get to first before anyone can make the throw.

The coach immediately replaces me with a pinch runner, sends me to the showers, except there isn't even a sink in our dugout. Instead of thinking, "Wow, it was my wish since I was a little kid to play pro baseball!" I'm more worried about how stupid I probably look on the replay, since I cringed at the thought of getting drilled with a 100 mph pitch, and that was probably going straight to YouTube. And as I leave the game, I'm also thinking about how this would mean I'd have a page on baseball-reference.com forever, with a 1.00 batting average.

After the at-bat, I'm talking to Pete Rose, who is selling hot dogs in the outfield behind first base. He tells me his strategy for shorting a NASDAQ index fund, and how it's going to make him millions, but he's selling hot dogs, so what the hell does he know. Someone asks him to sign a bratwurst in ketchup, and it reminds me of that place Tony Packo's in Toledo, which has walls filled with hot dog buns autographed by famous people. He asks the kid for a fifty-dollar signing fee, and when his parents pay it, he pockets the money and then refuses to sign in ketchup, because he's one of those assholes who holds a firm mustard-only stance on hot dog condiments.

\* \* \*

A group of freaks from the traveling show at the county fair are going door-to-door selling Girl Scout cookies: the bearded lady, the tattooed man, a sword swallower, someone who said he had the second-largest goiter in the southern hemisphere. The goiter really bothers me, and I can't even look at him; I tape twenty dollars to my front door and write "THIN MINTS" on the money. They take the cash and don't leave cookies, just a little comic book on how the Girl Scouts and the Pope are involved with the Church of Satan.

* * *

I'm in the basement of a church that was originally constructed as a ten-story Burger Chef cathedral, a brief experiment with fast food religion that bankrupted the chain back in the Seventies. I discover that if I focus my thoughts exactly, I can cause a fire engine to roar down the street with its sirens ablaze. I don't know if I'm starting fires telekinetically, or just causing false alarms or errant 911 calls. I figure if I get a police scanner radio and a little earphone, I could monitor the fire department radios, but I'm not sure if the walls of the church basement are shielded with metal to protect from nuclear fallout.

Hours later, I escape my mandatory religious instruction, and the Houston Oilers are running a bingo game in the parking lot. A seven-foot-tall albino with a bloody nose dumps bags of cedar shavings into a gas grill, causing an immense fire of toxic smoke. He breathes the smoke, laughs, and says he's stuck on jury duty all month, can't talk about the case, then spends ten minutes explaining every detail about the murder trial, how a guy allegedly killed his buddy in a coin-op car wash only a block away, then ran the body through every cycle of the machine: power rinse, soap, shampoo brush, rinse, wax, tire protectant.

The smoke is making my sinuses bleed, so I walk away, toward a set of railroad tracks behind the church. Two kids are jumping up and down on the greasy rails, trying to use them as a form of plyometric exercises. I have a perfect explanation of all the trigonometry involved in proving that this was a bad workout for your lower back, but I can't remember how to pronounce all the little math symbols, because I'd only read them in books. I then realize several of my upper teeth had been replaced with Phillips-head screws. When I run my tongue over them, it tastes like the terminals of a car battery.

Later, I'm in an all-night diner that only sells hot dogs, watching a moose walk down main street, like the opening credits of *Northern Exposure*, except I'm in Indiana. I ask the cashier if he saw the same thing, and he tells me to dial 1-800-EAT-SHIT. I write down the number and walk to a cold water flat where a friend of mine lives to use his pay phone. He rents a single room with a shared bathroom down the hall for twenty dollars a month, and all the utilities are free, but the electricity is on the 127-volt standard, like Madagascar. When I get to the building, it's now an empty lot, with a barbed wire fence around it, and a sign saying "THIS PROPERTY HAS BEEN REMOVED DUE TO DMCA COMPLAINT BY THE MCDONALDS CORPORATION."

I walk back to main street, and a parade is going through town, celebrating North Korea's triumphant victory over the United States. I want to cross the street, but a cop says I have to walk to the next town and use a railroad overpass. A John Deere tractor pulls a float with a cheerleader sitting on an anti-aircraft missile. She's throwing candy, and I get hit in the face with a yellow Starburst fruit chew.

\* \* \*

"Looks like Yoko Ono's pumpin' gas again." I stood outside a Circle K, chugging a tomato juice energy drink, talking to a guy who was filming passing cars with an old Super-8 movie camera from a garage sale. He says he wants to get the camera working, then throw it into the Grand Canyon. "I really wanted to fly spy planes, like in the army or whatever, but I guess you need math in high school now."

The summer heat broils the dried lake bed across the street. It looks like the last piece of pizza sizzling under the heat lamps at a Shakey's lunch bar, the molten cheese too hot to touch. The tomato juice is a bad idea. I need to inhale a dozen root beer floats, immediately. I go inside the Circle K to check the beverage situation, maybe get an IV of saline solution or a banana bag or whatever they give stroke victims.

The Pepsi-Cola Corporation started marketing a new beer-flavored slushie drink in select locations, like with malt-related vitamins in it, for strength. I don't know if it actually tastes like beer, or if it's some fake synthetic cotton candy flavor. I go to the machine and take a whiff of the spinning ice/fluid cylinders, and it smells like an empty keg of Michelob that sat on the front porch of a frat house for a week. No thanks.

\* \* \*

I'm trying to shop for bone saws in a Gimbel's catalog, not finding anything that looks durable enough for me, although I don't know why I need a bone saw. Daytime TV is droning on in the background. Jay Leno isn't a talk show host anymore; he's a judge on a TV court show, eating Doritos while people fight about property crime disputes. My neighbor comes over, dumps a hundred rolls of reel-to-reel tape on my kitchen counter, and says, "This contains the key to the Nixon presidency!" I tell him I have no way to play the tapes, and he tries to light them on fire with a stick of incense.

I drive to Little Caesar's pizza — because of some legal snafu, the only location in the state has to be thirty miles from any Pizza Hut or elementary school, so the takeout-only joint is in a swamp in the middle of nowhere. It's the area where the local FM stations have their hundred-foot towers, blasting high-watt signal across the airwaves. When I drive past the antennas, no matter what station I have tuned in, the broadcast feed from 107.7 The Bone rings through my entire car, vibrating the fillings in my teeth. I'm sure it's causing brain tumors, even though I don't believe that pseudoscience bullshit about power lines causing cancer. But I don't care, because I need that pizza.

I'm waiting for a pair of ham and cheese thin-crusts to come out of the oven, sucking down a paper pitcher of watered-down Coke. A portly greaser dude pulls up in a Ferrari 308 GTS, climbs out of the car window without opening the door. He's wearing a Harley shirt with blown-out sleeves and an Elvis belt buckle the size of a dinner plate, a likeness of The King stamped in cheap pewter. He tells the cashier that a volcano in Hawaii just blew, and we're all going to die, because the NORAD missile command's sensors are going to get jammed in volcano dust, and the computers will launch a pre-emptive strike against the Soviets, and they will retaliate. It sounds plausible, except the US missile system was built by the lowest bidder, so I don't expect it to work.

Fat Elvis buys all the leftover crazy bread in the store, hops back in his Ferrari and peels out. I notice it must be a kit car and not a genuine 308, because it barely spins the tires on gravel, and it has the unmistakable sound of a Volkswagen bug four-banger, that air-cooled plinking sound, like a cheap lawn tractor. I ask the cashier if he's heard about the Hawaii volcano thing, and he says he doesn't follow foreign news. "We are going to open some special events in here next month. Get a wine license. You know any bands who can play for free pizza? None of that devil rock shit though — owner's one of those religious assholes."

When I get the pizzas, it's snowing outside, an instant blanket of white, a foot of solid powder on the road, no hope in ever getting a snowplow in this backwater area. I drive with my left foot on the brake, the right foot on the gas, a tactic I read in a *GI Joe* graphic novel. The car slips sideways, but the steering still keeps it moving forward down the road, and this enables me to eat the pizza on the passenger seat while driving, which is a plus.

\* \* \*

I'm chugging lukewarm Sapporo beer from a silver, 18-sided can, because I read an ad in one of my ninja magazines that said it contains vitamin A and reduces kidney stones by 41%. I'm in the parking lot of an Econolodge, trying to take pictures of the moon with a Kodak disc camera taped to an old telescope. A security guard who looks like a fat ex-cop who got fired for leaving his gun in the bathroom of a donut shop keeps trying to explain to me that they could turn every abandoned Sears store into a storage facility for nuclear warheads, but he keeps saying nuh-cuh-lur, so I don't listen.

I go inside the motel lobby because a handwritten sign said they are selling new Mexican Fender Stratocasters in eighteen different sparkle colors for below list prices. A monkey in a top hat smoking a Winston hands me a copy of *Field and Stream* and a piece of birthday cake. It's a middle square from a generic sheet cake, no edge or corner frosting, no extra lettering or flowers on top, no fruit goo layer in the middle. I'm not even that impressed with the trained monkey, because the piece of cake is such bullshit. I throw both the cake and the magazine in the garbage and leave, completely forgetting about the guitars.

In the parking lot, the security guard is now talking to a prostitute in a bright green late-model Dodge Charger. He's still trying to sell someone on his Sears/nuclear silo theory. I slip by, and watch a 400-car freight train roll past at low speed. After trying to read the graffiti on the cars for at least an hour, I realize all the cars of the train had been organized in sequential order by car manufacture date, and it makes me wonder if we're all living in a computer simulation.

\* \* \*

I'm wandering through a medical conference which is made up of two types of booths: drug companies peddling the latest in pharmacological discoveries, and black-market researchers trying to sign up people to take illegal drugs to see what they do. The black marketers have much better swag. One of them is giving away brand new Apple watches if you sign a form you're not allowed to read first. I don't do it, but I see a lot of people with brand new Apple watches.

I talk to a woman dressed up as a random superhero, skin-tight leotard, but no distinguishing trademarks that could cause a lawsuit with Marvel or DC. I tell her I am interested in any allergy medication that would completely destroy my long-term memory, and make me into a zombie that could not determine it had no true purpose in life. She pulls out a suitcase that looks identical to the one Hunter S. Thompson/Johnny Depp had in *Fear and Loathing in Las Vegas*, and runs through the contents in a Depp-like voiceover, then hands me a small vial of pink pills. I'm excited to try them, but when I get to the parking lot and examine them, they're just Benadryl with a *Hello Kitty* label.

\* \* \*

I meet a guy with Whitesnake hair who lives in an abandoned 737 jet in the woods outside of town. He makes his living carving abstract metal sculptures of horses for hotel lobbies in the Southwest, but I'm there to see about a Boba Fett bass guitar he had listed in the Penny Trader. When I arrive at his place in the forest, he's outside, practicing ninja moves in a pair of leather pants with a full sword. He sweats profusely, and makes various whooping noises as he spins in the air with the blade.

"You ever notice how they only started getting shitty about that curtain between first class and coach after 9/11?" I am certain *Seinfeld* did a skit about this ten years earlier, but I keep my mouth shut. "It's like they think a piece of cloth can divide a country."

"Isn't that what flags do?"

"All I'm saying is if I've got a sword, I should be able to bring a sword on the plane. It's not a gun; it doesn't contain liquid. No luggage rules, no security checkpoints. I am doing them a service by carrying a blade. Fewer air marshals needed. And if someone has to open a plastic clam-shell package, I'm your guy. You smoke?"

"Like cigarettes?" I say.

"'Like cigarettes,'" he chuckles. "No, not like cigarettes." I then notice the entire forest we're standing in is made of marijuana plants. Some trees are forty, fifty feet tall. (I can't smell in the dream.) He pulls back a tarp, which I assumed was covering a cord of firewood, and reveals bundle after bundle of sinsemilla, with a street value of hundreds of thousands of dollars.

We laugh like we're in a bad sitcom, then drive into town on a United Airlines luggage cart, putting along the dirt road at three miles an hour. "Had a Japanese foreign exchange student up here two years ago. He didn't know much English — didn't know anything about sword construction either. Just sat around jerking off and playing video games. He got shot in the face on Halloween. Ol' Earl at the VFW saw him walking downtown in a *Star Wars* mask, thought it was the Japanese invasion. Earl served in the Philippines during the war, and I think it knocked a screw loose. Less than honorable discharge, something about drinking torpedo fuel. Unloaded his 1911 pistol in that kid's head. Cops let him go on a technicality though, castle doctrine. You ever drink torpedo fuel? I drank some turpentine on a dare once. Just like a quart of it. Wasn't bad once you got used to the aftertaste."

We go to a tiki bar owned by a guy on the practice squad of the Jacksonville Jaguars, and I get about two mai tais deep before I realize my car is still out at the guy's plane house. "Don't worry, this luggage cart practically drives itself. Have a beer, it'll help you sober up. It absorbs the alcohol." I go outside, vomit in the parking lot, then watch a pregnant woman argue with a guy who looks like Leo Tolstoy, something about General Robert E. Lee's effect on the home computer industry.

* * *

I'm in a Russian city, the one the game Tetris is based on. Large blocks are falling from the sky while that annoying song blasts through PA speakers all over town. I ask a cop where to eat lunch, and he hands me a paper map, circles a restaurant and tells me to go there for good sausages, but it's a map of Pyongyang from 1974. I wander the town square more, eat a roll of Tums antacid for the calories, and go to a throwback Soviet computer store.

Inside, a guy is trying to sell me a Bulgarian bootleg Apple II computer. He's dressed exactly like Steve Jobs, and says he's even got pancreatic cancer. I tell him he can save a lot of money if he always wears a rubber. He says he doesn't believe in birth control because he owns every Kraftwerk album.

I go to rent a snowmobile from a place that had Polaris machines and fried pirogies. The cashier spends twenty minutes telling me about all the various hotels in the city with ghost problems, then springs the news that their fryers were all broken and I'd have to eat boiled pirogies, which is bullshit.

\* \* \*

There's a Chinese vacation company calling my land line every five or ten minutes, an automated message saying I've won a free jet. After I start answering NO NO NO, a courier shows up at the house, telling me to sign a stack of papers that say my mortgage has a lien on it from someone with the last name NO. I know I'm going to spend the next year filing paperwork with the city to get this unfucked. I tell him he has the wrong timeline, and he needs to go back to the year 1972 in a reality in which the Houston Astros are always in the National League and Christopher Walken was in the first *Star Wars* movie. This confuses the courier enough that I'm able to escape.

I take an underground train across the country to New York. They've somehow expanded the MTA so it connects other city subways together, and you can transfer across local trains from San Francisco to Manhattan for $2.75, but it takes about two weeks. I'm working with a small team of computer programmers in a massive SoHo loft, no dividing walls and all open space, but it's got no lights, just candles and kerosene lanterns. We're developing on old classic Macintosh computers, platinum-colored beasts with big CRT monitors that weigh fifty or a hundred pounds. I can't remember at all how to use the MultiFinder on ancient Macs, let alone how to code using the Macintosh Programmer's Workshop.

The Mac I'm using has a screen like an old Philco Predicto TV set, a space-age pedestal tube of thick, wavy glass in an odd, rounded shape. It looks like a giant translucent amber cough drop lozenge on a chromed plastic base. Every time I start typing in the code editor, the screen warbles and flickers, like I'm looking through the porthole in a submarine into the deep water. A web browser in the background is streaming an episode of *The Drew Carey Show*, and after a few minutes, I realize it's filmed in a department store where I spent the night the week before when I missed one of my transfers somewhere in Ohio and had to wait for the next train.

The show is a three-hour long episode where all the characters are playing a *New York Times* crossword puzzle and free-associating about various fictional road trips. No commercial interruptions, sponsored by Metamucil. About twenty minutes in, I'm almost certain the characters are talking about a voyage I took in 1994 to Knoxville, Tennessee, but it wavers in and out of phase. I eat some grilled bison strips from a street vendor and I think they may be psychotropic, like they were basted in ketamine. The city banned labeling any foods, so I can't tell. I can't remember if an EpiPen is supposed to work for this, or if that's just for heroin overdoses.

Later, I'm driving a diesel Chevette in upstate New York, trying to find a comedy club somewhere near the Zoom Flume in East Durham. I stop at a gas station that sells personal pan pizzas. Everyone there is wearing clown makeup, and I can't tell if there is a Juggalo infestation in the area, or if Barnum and Bailey used to have a branch campus nearby. I consider calling the TSA and telling them, just in case, but I get distracted and buy a ten-pound bag of Combos pretzel snacks and a pony keg of Monster energy drink. They don't have diesel fuel, and tell me to drive to Canada for that shit.

Outside, a wiry kid with spiked hair is listening to AC/DC in a JC Penney jambox and shadow boxing. He looks like a Biafran starvation victim, but has fast feet, and a good left jab. He tells me he's going to fight Muhammed Ali someday, and I wonder how that's going to work, because he's been dead for years. Maybe that's his tactic.

* * *

I'm in a boat in Sloan Lake in Denver. It's a wooden rowboat, and I'm drilling holes in the bottom with a cordless power drill.

The drill bit is made of depleted uranium and is thinner than a human hair, so no water is coming through the holes. I wonder if I can drill into my own arm and not feel it, like when you accidentally cut yourself with a brand new X-Acto knife and it slices clean through the microscopic nerves. I'm afraid though that if I'm a secret Terminator robot and don't realize it, I'll drill through the outer flesh layer and hit a piece of titanium.

A Coast Guard riverboat pulls up to me, sirens blazing. It looks just like the boat in *Apocalypse Now*, but painted orange and with way more weapons. A guy in mirror shade glasses pulls out a bullhorn, and starts screaming three feet from my head. "MY BROTHER IS A CHRONIC BED WETTER. HE WANTS A JOB AT NASA BUT HE CAN'T DO SIMPLE ARITHMETIC. MY UNCLE TOLD HIM TO LEARN HOW TO WELD, BUT I THINK THEY HAVE ROBOTS DOING THAT NOW. WHAT'S WITH THE DRILL, BUDDY?"

I have no answer. I ask if I am being detained. He says no, so I row to shore, abandon the boat and drill, and walk to a Del Taco restaurant. There's nobody inside except a Pakistani guy blasting old Poison records and gluing Elvis postage stamps into a library book on the history of barbecue grills. When I go to look at the menu, he tells me to hold out my hands and cup them together. I do, and he pours hot nacho cheese into my palms. It's a bright orange, and it burns my skin like napalm.

I'm still licking away cheese as I walk through a mall that used to be the factory where they built stealth bombers or nuclear missiles or something. It's about ten million square feet, and many of the stores are duplicates. Like it has four Apple stores, and ten Hot Dog on a Stick locations. I'm not really hungry, but I get a pretzel for emergency purposes, and lay down in a king-sized bed in one of the two dozen mattress shops.

I fall asleep, and enter another dream, about buying a Toto album as a goof, and throwing it in the garbage because a hard bop jazz trumpet player made fun of all music with lyrics. We drive to a Pizza Hut somewhere in southern Michigan, next to an abandoned paper factory that was now used for indefinite detention of terrorists and illegal immigrants. He's got an old Honda Civic that's covered from stem to stern with bumper stickers for Ross Perot and Butt Drugs. The dream within a dream is in black and white, because the guy is telling me about the bright red of his *Star Trek* uniform, and it looks gray to me. Somewhere outside of Niles, Michigan, we stop for a drink at a fake old-time saloon that has a model train running around the perimeter, delivering drinks in mason jars.

The tavern is out of Diet Coke, so I get a vanilla soda, but it tastes like hand soap. I look at it under a flashlight and realize the glass is covered in Dawn dishwashing detergent, and I start vomiting, and then wake up back into the first dream, where I'm still vomiting, and think about the implications of an inter-dream stream of vomit, like if there would be a way for scientists to use a spectrograph to measure the connection to the other world through the amount of bile and undigested food in my puke. I try to write this down in a letter to Stephen Hawking, but then wake up from both dreams and realize he's dead, and he probably never puked much because of his paralysis or whatever he had going on.

* * *

I leave my job in the middle of a shift, smash my cell phone into pieces, and wander the desert to have a long, hard look at my life so far, think about my mistakes and maybe what I could change in my diet to lower cholesterol without actually quitting anything. I don't wear a shirt in the desert, didn't think of sunscreen, and fixate on the idea of catching cancer and dying from severe dehydration. My back and arms look like the surface of Venus, feel like a coarse-grain sandpaper with a very low grit number, like single digits.

I keep thinking about how house flipping is basically legalized necrophilia, and we are all grave-robbing the dead for some jollies by destroying craftsman homes and blowing out walls to make open concept kitchens. I wonder if ketamine injections would fix my brain so I would stop thinking. It's how they get horses to act groovy, even though they know they're one broken leg away from a life of glue. My podiatrist says he could hook me up with the special K trip, but it sounds a bit dodgy. He went to a religious school where Jim Jones spoke at his commencement, and this was twenty years after Jonestown.

* * *

TV is now mandatory, like North Korea, except it isn't even free — you're required pay $200 a month for cable, and keep a set in every room turned on at all times, or else. TV cops roam the poor neighborhoods, busting anyone without a constant news feed pumping into their living room. Cord-cutters are now felons, a drain on society. All hail God Emperor, or spend a year in federal prison!

The clone debate rages on in the news, some rich asshole making copies of himself and hunting them from a helicopter from a sniper rifle. "If anything, I should be charged with suicide, not murder, and that's not illegal. Having sexual relations with my own clones is technically masturbation, not sodomy. Killing a clone is like cutting off a wart, only bigger. Go arrest Kirk Cobain, you fucks. I pay taxes!" I know in a week, he'd either be dead or a State Senator.

I fall asleep in front of the boob tube, and in the dream, wonder why we still called it a tube, even though they stopped making the vacuum-filled cathode rays twenty years ago. I think I slept better back when I had a two-hundred pound Trinitron across the room, burning hundreds of watts of power, shooting radioactive light into the atmosphere. In the days of a console with a piece of glass a yard across, I barely ran the heater in my apartment, unless it dipped down into like North Dakota temps.

Some wildlife show flows across the screen while I dream of a crusty old man performing cosmetic surgery on blue whales, lancing basketball-sized pustules with a machete the size of a broom. They leak pus like a fire hydrant, and I remember a time when my rotting wisdom teeth went septic, infected, oozing a green-white discharge. This didn't happen in real life, just a recurring dental trauma nightmare, the kind that made me wish Quaaludes were still legal and I could find a shrink that was loose with the prescription pad.

Mr. Curry from the apartment across the hall had his spinal discs removed that week, replaced with hockey puck-shaped slabs of polyurethane, originally designed as frame bushings for a 1980s Trans Am. They did the surgery in a temporary VA clinic opened in an old Pontiac dealership out by the mall, using as many of the car dealer's spare parts as possible. They wheeled him in the car lift area they repurposed as an OR, with the oil change hoses now pumping morphine, propofol, and raw saline. After the surgery, they sprayed him down with new car smell as a disinfectant. The surgery worked, but now every time he moves, I can hear the squeaking of the synthetic resin bushings between his bones. He sounds like a car suspension that needs a lube job. I have to wear earplugs and run the shower all night to sleep.

Something startles me outside, the crash of a car falling onto the sidewalk, its wheels stolen from under it. I am two hours into a PBS documentary on making cheese out of whale milk, and they hadn't even shown any of the cheese yet. It has Jacques Cousteau's crusty French neighbor talking to an Orca with a modified Speak and Spell, trying to explain the concept of brie with one-syllable words. The Texas Instrument toy must have been an export version because the synthesized voice has a thick French accent.

* * *

The discount airline loads me on a tiny commuter micro-jet, a Buddy Holly thing built in the Soviet Union that barely flies above the speed limit. And they charge me $80 to carry my wallet on the plane. I didn't even bring luggage — I hope to buy three of everything at Target when I get there, throw it all in the garbage before flying home.

Ten minutes after take-off, the copilot announces he has to take a dump, and they only have a plastic Fisher-Price crapper in the back of the plane. Even when clean and sanitized, it smells worse than the porta-potty at a hippy jam band festival on the third day. The pilot says there's no way they can make it back to O'Hare, and the copilot is cramping up something fierce. The crew calls in a terrorism, diverts the flight and lands on a county road in the middle of Iowa. I hear all of this, because the plane is about as big as a Volkswagen Rabbit and has no wall dividing the cabin from the cockpit.

The copilot makes a run for the unisex bathroom behind a Marathon gas station, and has a total career-ending bowel movement that is so bad, it shows up on the Weather Channel's automated sensor banks, made it look like a micro-storm was destroying a nearby village. While he's in there dominating it, the plane's landing gear sinks in the chip-seal pavement of the road. Even those tiny turboprop pieces of garbage can weigh twenty, thirty tons once you get 'em fueled up and filled with obese passengers and their 17 items of carry-on luggage.

We have to wait fourteen hours for them to rent a school bus and shuttle everyone into the next real city. And then the airline claims that the Taco Bell Diarreto the pilot dude ate was an Act of God and they don't have to give us free motel rooms. I sleep in the luggage area of the airport, where some genius dropped fifty pounds of spaghetti into the luggage carousel. Can you imagine how hard it is to clean marinara sauce out of the moving parts of those conveyors? They're probably still picking meat out of that machine.

\* \* \*

I'm stuck in a Pink Floyd music video from that shitty album in the late Eighties, the one that doesn't have any of the original members in it. I've somehow been given an electronic implant in my left arm. It feels like one of those Norplant birth control things. It has a flashing red light and it beeps every 187 seconds, the loud chirp of a smoke detector with a bad battery.

I go to Radio Shack to buy tools to remove it, but they only sell waterbeds and disco lights. I wonder when they still sold radios — was that in the Fifties? Sixties? Way before my time. I ask for a free battery card and a cashier in suede and denim tries to sell me some Quaaludes. He says they're totally non-addictive, right before he falls into a coma.

\* \* \*

There's a black oil leaking through the cracks in the laminate flooring of every room in my apartment. I sniff the ooze, and it has the strong odor of raw sewage. It's happening in rooms nowhere near the bathroom, and there's a three-foot-thick concrete slab below the thin layer of fake wood, so it can't be buried pipes or broken plumbing. I imagine the worst, a pool of fermented excrement underneath the entire house, slowly leaking up by capillary action. I might as well burn the place to the ground now, before someone calls it in to the EPA and I'm liable for cleaning up the entire neighborhood.

I go to the bathroom to see if the sewage is originating from there. The sink is on the ground in pieces; the toilet is completely missing, with only a flange pipe to the septic system bolted to the floor. I think maybe an earthquake or volcano caused it, but I don't remember if one happened overnight. I know there's a web site that tells you if an earthquake occurred, but when I try to find it on Google, only sites about Amish cheese come up. When I add "-amish -cheese" to my search, my browser immediately crashes, and restarts my computer. I repeat this ten times, same thing.

When I call the plumber to replace the broken fixtures, he tells me he's busy all month, watching a pornographic documentary on the San Francisco Giants. He explains to me on the phone how I can fix any sewage in the garbage disposal, by disassembling everything and using a special Torx wrench to operate a manual control on the bottom. I spend the next three days disassembling the InSinkErator, and find a severed finger and a wedding ring wrapped around one of the blades inside.

I've lived in the apartment ten years, and I know it isn't my finger, didn't happen under my watch.

At the fire station down the road, I throw the finger in the baby drop-off box, so maybe someone will claim it and reattach it, if that's possible. On the way home, I'm distracted by a sale at the Eat-a-Pita. They are selling falafel-flavored mechanical keyboards for half price, Tuesdays only. I don't need one, but it's a good deal, and Christmas is only ten months away.

* * *

I'm trying to drink an entire swimming pool filled with cream soda to set a world record. I'm not really a fan of cream soda, and this one has a sickly artificial vanilla flavor to it that tastes like candle wax. It's also warm, which makes it taste worse. But a record is a record, and I need to do something with my life. I sit in the deep end of the pool, treading water and drinking as much as possible between each breath, watching the side of the pool to see if the level is lowering at all.

I chug about an inch of the pool height, then climb out and wash the syrup and sugar in the poolside shower, which is almost freezing, but the temperature outside is like a hundred degrees that afternoon, so it's not bad. I go to the front yard, and every house on the street looks like the plantation mansion from *Gone With the Wind*. I try not to throw up, but vomit profusely in the driveway while a family of Mormons playing Pac-Man on an Atari 5200 in their living room watch me.

* * *

Typical nightmare about not knowing I'm registered for a class until the day of the midterm, and I have to take it cold — this really happened to me a few times, most notably in a Calculus III class, so it comes up a lot. This time, it's a self-surgery class, and I have to cut off and reattach at least three of my own fingers. I've never done more than minor pimple-popping or mole removal before, and don't know the names of the various tendons and nerves and other garbage in there, let alone how to reattach them. I write "NO" on a piece of paper, turn it in, and leave.

It's a beautiful spring day out, sunny and warm, but the thousand acres of campus is populated exclusively with ginkgo trees. They're all dropping their walnut-looking fruit, which smells horrific, like putrefying flesh drenched in rancid butter. I read in a book somewhere that the only trees that survived at Hiroshima and Nagasaki were ginkgo, which makes me think about how only cockroaches will survive the nuclear war.

I breathe through my mouth, and walk to a campus bookstore, where Foghat is playing an impromptu acoustic set. They have just released an album of Iron Maiden covers done as R&B slow jams, and are twenty minutes into an hour-long rendition of "Seventh Son of a Seventh Son." Dave Peverett does not have the vocal range of Bruce Dickinson, but then again he's been dead for almost twenty years, and he's standing right in front of me belting out Iron Maiden at quarter-speed, so none of it makes sense.

I fall asleep on a couch in the student union and drift into a dream-within-a-dream about stealing an old Corvette ZR-1 piece-by-piece from someone's garage, and hiding all the parts in the space between the drop ceiling and the roof of a two-screen theater that had been converted into a gospel church. I sneak into the cavern by popping a ceiling tile above the concession stand and climbing upward with a grappling hook. I can't determine how big the cavern was, so I bring a hundred feet of carbon-fiber cable, tie one end to a structural support, and go spelunking with a *Little Mermaid* flashlight, trying to find the outer boundaries of the space. I easily climb a hundred feet without stopping, then repeat the experiment with five miles of phone wire. It is some kind of trans-dimensional hole — the building itself is maybe only fifty feet wide, but the space continues for miles in every direction. I have to walk on the narrow metal grids between the tiles, for fear of stepping through the thin ceiling, and there's also the constant fear of getting caught by a redneck security guard with a gun.

I don't remember how this continues, except I wake up screaming in the original dream, and the couch I'm sleeping on is now covered in bedbugs, which are drilling into my skin like an Alfred Hitchcock horror movie about insects. As I scratch the welts and insects, I realize my hands are covered in oil from the ginkgo fruits, which is basically like poison ivy juice, and I'm now grinding it into every inch of my already-raw skin. Then I actually wake up, and have to take a shower for 45 minutes to convince myself it didn't happen.

\* \* \*

It's a Japanese bank holiday, and only the bars and gas stations are open. I'm at a place called "FUCKY TAVERNS" and I'm starving. I'm standing at a side table filled with gold-plated short ribs. (Well, they're not plated — it's more like they're encrusted, or rolled in gold dust so it adheres to the sauce.) When I dig in, the gold dust fills my sinuses, tastes like licking the blood of a freshly-killed horse.

The bartender's hair is an uncomfortable and unnatural shade of magnesium, poorly framing her neck tattoos of Grateful Dead bears and Burger King Kids' Club characters. The tats look more like hickeys or bruises than tattoos. She wears rubber boots like a fisherman and talks about how her life was ruined because her prom date twenty years ago bought the wrong color corsage.

I want to order some Kobe beef sliders and onion rings, but she tells me they are only served on weekends. The kitchen is on one of those nights-and-weekends cooking gas plans, and can only microwave stuff for lunch. I ask about cold tacos, and she assumes I mean necrophilia and calls the police. But the band The Police shows up, and I end up talking to Stewart Copeland for an hour about how he played drums on that one Peter Gabriel album.

\* \* \*

I'm hitchhiking across Nevada and get picked up by an asshole in an old Audi 5000 that smells like curry and burned motor oil.

He's trying to visit every Foot Locker store in America, and financing it with a counterfeit money order machine. I have a stack of finger sandwiches made from bologna and cheddar cheese, cut into circles, stored in a Pringles canister. I'm starving and want to eat a sandwich or ten, but the oil smell is horrendous.

I remember that the corporation now known as Foot Locker is actually the same company that used to be Woolworth's the century before. I want to bring this up, but the guy won't shut the fuck up about how he's trying to buy a limited-edition pair of Nike Air Jordans that were made for Kim Jong-Un. I personally know Kim Jong-Un (in the dream, at least) and know Dear Leader can't wear tennis shoes because of numerous ankle injuries, but I don't mention this, because it's obvious the guy isn't listening.

We stop at a road house in the middle of nowhere, fifty miles from anything in the desert. It's a gas station and brothel, with a small stage where a stand-up comedian who looks exactly like Gilbert Gottfried is chain smoking and reading from a phone book into a Radio Shack microphone plugged into a five-watt guitar amp. I sit at a table with the Audi driver and we order five pounds of flaming-hot nachos and a pitcher of Mello Yello.

While we're eating nachos covered in a volcano cheese sauce and my hands and face are becoming more and more orange, the driver offers to buy me a prostitute at the dude ranch. But of the five women working the crowd, the most attractive one looks like the Algerian lunch lady at my elementary school, who was an Olympic shotputter before she defected to America. After she died, it turned out she was biologically a male, or was intersex, or maybe the steroids made her grow a pair, I don't really know. (Not that there's anything wrong with that. And yes, I'm probably pronouning this wrong. Sorry.) I'm getting increasingly sick from all the hot peppers I'm consuming, and know this will end with me shitting my pants in the desert.

The comedian drops the mic on the ground and it feeds back loudly. He marches off to the parking lot and shoots heroin ironically. Another guy, dressed like one of the cowboys in the Devo video for "Whip It" comes up to the stage with an acoustic guitar from Sears that has never been tuned, ever. He plays the first four bars of "Carry on My Wayward Son," then pauses, freezes, and starts the song from the beginning. He does this over and over, at least a dozen times. I try to wipe the nacho sauce from my hands and face with a lemon-scented wet-nap, but I realize even if I had a dozen of them, I'd still be a mess, and I know it's only a matter of moments before I try to adjust a contact lens and deposit a gram of pure capsaicin on my eyeball.

The driver says if we leave now, we can make it to Belgium by midnight, which makes no sense, unless there's a Belgium, Nevada, and I don't want to look it up and get cheese and hot sauce on my phone. I ask if we can get some nachos to go, and he says no, because he doesn't allow people to eat in his car, which makes no sense, because the Audi basically smells like the deep fryer in a shitty restaurant. We get back in the car, and it unintentionally accelerates into the back of someone's jeep while we're still in park.

* * *

I'm at an A&W hot dog stand in the Netherlands, chugging a gallon of super-sweet root beer from a plastic jug. A cashier who looks like one of the guys from *Jersey Shore* is screaming at me about how the Sacramento levee infrastructure is woefully under-engineered. The hot dogs rolling under the warming lights are struggling, wiggling like worms, trying to get free. I remember an article about someone who got microscopic hookworms growing in their eyeballs from mosquito bites, and I have to immediately put my genitals in a blender to not think about parasites eating my eyes.

The terror-stress makes me break into a fever, night sweats, a ten-day sickness that no cough medicine could cure. My circadian rhythms go sideways; I sleep twenty hours, eat a gallon of soup, fall asleep again for an hour, repeat the cycle. My dreams become reality. And then when I wake from those dreams, I'm still in the first dream, driving a rental car through Amsterdam, trying to remember what side of the street they drove on while prostitutes in storefront windows yelled at me, screaming that they now take Apple Pay.

* * *

I'm at an old IGA grocery store, looking at all the jars of pickled foods in aisle 7. Next to the brined cucumbers, onions, and peppers, I find a gallon-sized jar of pickled human penises. I read the label, and in large print, it says "GUARANTEED: NO CRIMINALS." I think about buying a jar to keep around the house for laughs, like the bottle of Vegemite spread I keep on the living room table as a conversation piece. But I'm afraid the container will bust open and I'll end up with pickled sex organ juice all over the place.

I go to the next aisle, and find it's a wormhole into a collection of products from the past and future. There are foods with expiration dates of 2048, video chip implants of movies that haven't come out yet, parts for flying speeder cars. I also find a bottle of cooking sherry from 1927 that says "NOW CONTAINS OPIUM!" on the label. I know this was the premise of a Philip K. Dick book, but I don't remember which one. I look for a magazine rack, hoping for a stock market newspaper or a sports scores book, but only find celebrity gossip rags, and I can't recognize any of the celebrities. (Although, to be honest, that happens with present-day paparazzi magazines, too.)

I buy a can of spray cheese and some baked crackers (trying to stay healthy) then walk to a valley between two sides of a highway, where there are a cluster of Easter Island-style big head statues, except all the heads are Richard Nixon. It's a good place to sit in the grass and eat cheese and crackers, except right after I sit down, a guy who looks like Danny DeVito comes over and starts telling me about how he's a champion pool player, but he's been banned from all United States Professional Poolplayers Association events and competitions because he broke into

Arnold Palmer's vacation home in 1974 and replaced the toilet paper with sandpaper. "And why is toilet paper two words and sandpaper one word? If you really think about it, the only difference is the grit." The more the man talks, the more I realized he probably was Danny DeVito.

I give him the cheese and crackers, and walk to a geodesic dome convention center that's holding a regional science fair. It's filled with drunken Naval officers who are placing bets on which kid's vinegar/baking soda volcano would explode the most. I think about laying down a five-buck long-shot bet, just in case, but none of the Navy guys will talk to me. I study one kid's project on enhanced interrogation chemicals, until a neurotic high school teacher comes up and starts screaming that torture is never funny.

It's suddenly important to me that I know if the geodesic building's floor plan is round or hexagonal. I walk the perimeter of the building and eyeball each angle, thinking if I could divide 360 by the angle, I could determine the number of sides. But the sides are curved. (I later look it up on Google Maps, and it's more or less a pentagon shape, but with the outer walls having a slight arc, like maybe if the Chrysler logo gained twenty pounds.)

Danny DeVito shows up at the science fair, wearing a baby carrier that's filled with french fries, double-fisting Big Macs, a sandwich in each hand. He's telling me about how a Moose Lodge downtown has a bowling alley that has free nachos on Thursdays, but I can barely understand a word he's saying, because he's spitting all-beef patties, special sauce, lettuce, cheese, and chunks of sesame seed bun in a ten-foot radius.

\* \* \*

The only business open in the little hippy tourist town is a health food shop that sells vegan lemonade for five bucks a shot. It is 110 degrees out and must be in the mountains, high elevation, so my nose is bleeding and I need something to drink, immediately. I buy a dixie cup full of fresh-squeezed juice, and the cashier, who looks exactly like Tommy Chong, scrutinizes my tennis shoes, looking for any leather content. I tell him they used to belong to Phil Lesh, and he nods in agreement.

The trivia night at the bar and grill next door got shut down by the local police. Their all-you-can-eat Stromboli plate had chunks of reindeer in it. Wasn't even organic. They wanted to burn the place down with torches, but that's a big carbon footprint. Burning one log in a fireplace is like running a car all year with no exhaust. And solar tiki torches haven't really been worked out yet.

I want to shoot high-speed film footage of a nuclear explosion and eat pickled eggs straight from the jar. I don't want to put on sunscreen, because I know I will get it in my eye. The cashier asks me why I'm hauling around a huge Anvil case filled with camera gear. I tell him it's guitar gear I stole from Mötley Crüe and I need to throw it in a volcano or everyone on earth will become color blind and the Pantone corporation gave me an unlimited Visa card and Meg Ryan's boat if I'd do it. He nods, and goes back to squeezing lemons.

Jets keep flying overhead, fighter jets, full afterburner at military power. I don't know if it's a military exercise, a terrorist threat, or just an air show. It makes me think of the game *Afterburner*, and how I spent a semester of college on a heavy dose of antidepressants, which made me overly compulsive. I did nothing but shovel my tuition into arcade machines, playing *Smash TV* for hours. Dopamine imbalance — there's a lawsuit on this, but I didn't lose enough money to qualify. Still ended up losing my scholarship, though.

"These fucking trolley tracks to nowhere need to go," said the cashier. "I know we're supposed to worship transit workers now, but train operators in the city are getting paid two hundred grand a year to push a button once an hour. Last time I was in the city for the hemp convention, I saw a guy watching a pornography on one of those tablet things. An escaped prisoner was slashing peoples' throats and stealing their camcorders and whatnot, and he's not paying attention, too busy with Nurse Nancy. We need to replace everyone with robots, me included. Buy a Juiceman Juicer, plug it into one of those Nest thermostats, and give me basic income. And legal weed."

I don't know what train tracks he's talking about. I go outside again, call a buddy in the Air Force collect on a pay phone, and tell him about the jets. He laughs, tells me he flies drones now in North Dakota, and is going to use his GI Bill to study feng shui. "There's no future in technology, but if I can get paid a hundred bucks an hour to tell someone where to put their couch, count me in."

\* \* \*

I'm trying to eat a foot-long hot dog in a Barnes and Noble parking lot, but it's fifty below zero out, and blood is dripping from my eyeballs. Someone sends me a text in Chinese. I paste it into Google Translate, and it says something like "I'm dying on a picnic bench in Truth or Consequences, New Mexico, and my pet alpaca is running in a primary election in the fall." I'm not sure if it's a political spam, or a plea for help.

\* \* \*

In the dream, I remember another dream, or maybe a blackout drunk episode, where I wander a desolate part of West Seattle and get picked up by two teenage Mexican girls in a Ford Fiesta who laugh like criminal drug addicts and offer me part of a burrito with french fries and Almond Joy candy bars in it. Both girls have no eyebrows, shaved clean off and redrawn with magic marker, which reminds me of an old internet BBS where people would post pictures of how many sharpies they could shove in their butthole. They say they are in MS-13, but just for the roadside assistance benefits.

One of the girls, who was the less attractive of the two, explains to me that she uses a secret spy marker that she got from a grocery store to draw on her eyebrows, and if she meets the right person as her soulmate, they will have an antidote marker, which they can rub on her face and alter her fake eyebrows, thereby changing her facial expression. I want to ask her if she ever showered, because I remember in the movie *Showgirls*, Elizabeth Berkeley blew Agent Dale Cooper in the swimming pool and then came out with absolutely perfect makeup. I'm not saying I had a complete suspension of disbelief up to this point in the movie, but my sense of realism in the film was thrown by that scene.

I'm not sure if this was an actual blackout drunk episode I'm remembering inside the dream, or it's another previous dream, or a dream I manufactured inside the other dream, if that makes any sense. I remember, after waking up, trying to determine when the worst of my blackouts were during my time in Seattle, to see if reality lined up with the dreamscape, but that was so long ago, and most of my alcohol abuse didn't involve any long-range foot patrols, just stomping around my apartment in a shame spiral and sending incoherent email to ex-girlfriends which I wish I could now retroactively delete, or maybe read aloud as a performance piece at an alt-comedy festival and get a book deal.

That vision setting recurs frequently, and makes me wonder if the other side of my consciousness contained a set number of stages in which I interacted, or if this was an area I can't remember in reality. I didn't spend much time in West Seattle back in the day — I remember several trips to a shop that sold overpriced German melee weapons made of brass and copper to the everyday carry crowd, tactical clubs and batons and whatnot.

I never bought anything, but the window shopping was a good way to kill a Saturday when it was 40 degrees and raining and dark and suicidal outside.

Another frequent stage was some forgotten, half-dead mall, a place that resembled an amalgam of a few places I'd seen after the Peak Mall years. I'd often exit a highway or turnpike in the middle of nowhere in Ohio or Pennsylvania or upstate New York, and scout out the retail operations. I'd buy a large fountain drink at a Wawa gas station, ask the attendant what the pussy game was around town, then drive to an abandoned shopping center and see if their indie record store still existed. Enough of these sad plazas, with drained fountains and dead ferns in brick planters, became imprinted in my brain that they'd always come back in my sleep. The dreams would distort and rearrange the distant memories of the malls, preserving addled versions of them long after they'd been demolished and replaced with big-box chain restaurants offering endless low-quality pasta to senior citizens.

I remember a mall in a dream — at least I think it was a dream — where an anchor store, previously a Lazarus or May department store, sold nothing but taxidermied mice arranged in dioramas for various holidays. Like there were Christmas manger displays, with a baby mouse Jesus, a few stuffed hamsters as wise men, etc. This was in rural Iowa or West Virginia or some forgotten rust belt city, and there was enough store traffic to normalize the sale of hand-crafted displays for dead animals. I briefly wondered if the artisans bought the rodent corpses or caught them in traps.

The dream mall didn't have a parking lot — it sat on a river, or had a protective moat, or straddled a fault line, some foundation-related confusion that was never fully explained, but was generally accepted. It was like cell phone technology: everyone knew it worked, but nobody knew how it worked. (Satellites? Towers? Radios? Radio stations? Internet? And what happened to the antennas? You used to have to whip out a little antenna, walkie-talkie-style to make calls. Now cell phones were little rectangles with no protruding parts whatsoever.)

\* \* \*

The mayor of Chicago — or maybe the Governor of Illinois — bulldozed all seven runways at O'Hare airport in the middle of the night, scratching the word "LOL" in the asphalt in hundred-foot letters, so no planes could take off or land. It was about an argument with the state of Indiana or the toll road or something — he got loaded at that Harry Caray steakhouse out in Rosemont, went berserker when they wouldn't make him a porterhouse well-done, and started drunk dialing every government official in his phone, telling them to do insane and destructive shit.

Because the rental car situation at the airport is now broken, I'm trying to drive a Zamboni from Hammond to O'Hare, and keep getting cut off in traffic. The top speed of an ice resurfacer is about nine miles an hour with the blade turned off, but gridlock is so horrible, I can't even do that. I spend most of the drive reading a Zamboni catalog, and am surprised they make a machine called the "Black Widow" which is used to push dirt into graves at cemeteries. I think about how cool it would be to put Peavey Black Widow bass speakers in a truck called the Black Widow.

\* \* \*

I start getting texts from a guy in the hospital who broke his neck in a fight with a sign language monkey at the zoo. I reply to his texts "WRONG NUMBER WRONG NUMBER" but he keeps sending me pictures of his hospital food and all-caps ramblings about how he's going to sue the monkey in a court in Switzerland because they recognize ape personhood. His doctor put him on a vegan diet because he weighs 500 pounds and he's ten seconds from a massive coronary. He keeps trying to convince me that steaks are vegan because they don't come from animals; they come from grocery stores.

I drive to the mall to change my phone number, but the guy at the cell phone store tells me I bought it at a non-franchise location and I have to drive to Reno to get a new one. I ask him if I can just call them, and he tells me I bought it at a non-franchise location. I ask him what a franchise location is, and he asks me for my phone IMEI, even though he's holding the phone in his hand. I tell him I don't know what it is and he tells me I probably bought it at a non-franchise location.

It takes me ten days to drive to Reno, because they've changed the speed limit on highways to thirty miles an hour unless you own an American car, and even American cars are made in China now. The cell phone store is closed permanently; a sign on the door says "NOT A FRANCHISE LOCATION." I get a dozen more texts with pictures of hospital chicken con carne, and when I block the phone number, he gets a new burner phone and starts texting again.

\* \* \*

I'm sitting at a bus stop with an ex-girlfriend from college, and she doesn't remember me, even though we dated for like three or four years and were supposed to get married. She's telling me about how she volunteers at a zoo that brings special needs animals to the opera. I have a laptop in my backpack, and I know it has all of our email correspondence from back in the day, and I debate showing it to her to prove... something, I don't know what. But I figure she'd think I was psycho instead of sentimental, and I never should tell anyone anything about anything anymore.

I take the bus to the bombed-out part of the city where my friend Frank lives, in a squat that used to be a tuxedo shop like before the war. It's got mannequins in the windows, but they all have no clothes and are wrapped in duct tape so they look like background actors in a Sixties b-movie that takes place on the planet Jupidor in the year 1993. Frank got into drugs big-time in high school, spent a few years in prison for beating the shit out of a mall cop in some Spencer's-related disagreement. But now he's clean, lifts weights constantly, listens to the Joe Rogan podcast, and is totally ripped. He's still got a goofy nerd-looking head, though. He looks like if you put Dwight Schrute's head on Henry Rollins, but with more tattoos.

When I get to Frank's, there are cameras and tripods everywhere. He's doing curls with a hundred pounds of chromed barbells on his front porch. He tells me he's hired the entire cast from a community theater production of *Brigadoon*, and he's going to film them fucking and sucking each other while in costume. He says he has permission from the Alan Jay Lerner Estate to use the likenesses from the musical, but I don't believe him. Frank can be a bit of a liar. He told everyone in high school he was related to Ralph Macchio. He also told people his father invented the Post-It note by accident.

I tell Frank about the ex-girlfriend and his only advice to me is to "follow my dreams." He also tells me about how he found an imitation leather jacket with the Pontiac Fiero logo on it at the Goodwill, and now he only needs to buy the car. None of the cast members are at the house yet — they're all at an Alcoholics Anonymous meeting, or maybe a Toastmaster's class — so I tell Frank I have to run. I go to a coin-operated car wash and put five dollars of Armor All on my shoes, so I can light them on fire without burning myself. (I saw this on David Letterman.)

* * *

At Disassociated Foods — a woman who looks like Wayne Gretzky refuses to sell me Kingsford lighter fluid because she's Jewish and it's after sundown on Friday. I ask to see a manager, and she tells me her father designed the failed *2001: A Space Odyssey* rollercoaster at the Tampa Busch Gardens. I remember riding it, years after the Kubrick estate sued the theme park to remove his name from the project. They repainted the ride in tan camouflage and said it was a tribute to the heroes of Operation Desert Storm, but it wasn't that exciting, and smelled like canned meat for some reason.

"They used expired hot dogs to lube the drive chains," she says. "They would feed the leftovers from the old Houlihan Stadium concession stands to the alligators, but the world wildlife people made them stop. And it's too expensive to ship 'em to Guantanamo. I don't even know if the Taliban eats hot dogs. Maybe if they're beef." She gets out an abridged dictionary and starts showing me pictures of maritime flags, saying it's the only way she can communicate with her neighbor's kid, who has a brain disorder from drinking bottled water. I ask her if maybe the kid was drinking straight distilled water, and she starts screaming that I'm an ableist and don't understand.

* * *

The temperature of the earth is rising by like a degree per day every day, and the government has fully legalized the use of asbestos clothing. I watch the six o'clock news, and the anchormen have bright orange blazers made with thick layers of the carcinogenic flame-resistant insulation. They tell us to go to the local Woolworth's and buy, buy, buy. I already know from my extensive *Twilight Zone* binge-watching that this is a dream, and when I wake up, the planet is going to be drifting away from the sun and we'll freeze to death.

I go to Walmart to see if they are selling rip-off asbestos coats, and Lou Diamond Phillips is doing an in-store promo for a two-CD didgeridoo album he's just released. "All the money goes to the indifferent people of Australia!" During the Q&A session, I ask him if he means "indigenous people" and he said no, indifferent is the correct use of the word, then he tells a story about how he drinks Gatorade because the potassium content makes him invisible to drone airplanes.

At the snack bar outside the Walmart, two kids in Slayer shirts are cooking frozen pizza on a sidewalk. They get in a fistfight about whether New York or Chicago pizza is better, and it develops into a riot where twenty-three people are killed. I want a hot dog or ten, but it's not worth the risk of death, so I walk through a fake town like the ones North Korea builds on the DMZ until I find a Carl's Jr. and end up with food poisoning.

\* \* \*

I steal towels from the hotel because they have the name and address on them, and I can use them to find my way back home after I get blackout drunk that evening. The pre-party consists of eating six roast beef sandwiches while watching a Cindy

Crawford action-adventure movie that must have been direct-to-video, during that brief period of the Nineties where she thought she could act. I am eating the sandwiches and scribbling down romantic haiku as written by Timothy McVeigh — lots of stuff about getting busy in the back of a Ryder truck, and fertilizer.

It's one of the nicest hotels in Cambridge, but it's crawling with rats under the beds and in the walls. I call down to the front desk to ask for some mouse traps, and they say it's the anniversary of the alleged death of Marilyn Monroe and they can't leave the phones. I ask about glue traps and the guy laughs at me, tells me there's no way to get high off those. I hold up the phone to the sounds of a thousand rats cackling and scurrying, but he hangs up. Before I can call back, the rodents chew through the phone cord.

When I leave for the party, I tape shut the windows and door, and fill the room with carbon monoxide from a scuba tank. (Not sure why I was carrying a tank of pressurized CO, but maybe I should start doing that from now on.) A cabbie who looks like Lyndon LaRouche takes me to the wrong convention hall, a place filled with medical executives and drug salespeople dressed as slutty Amish women. The only food there is sugary cheesecake with no topping and bowls of little red Sudafed tablets.

The decongestant tablets go down like peanuts, handfuls at a time, until I realize I've probably eaten a pound of pure ephedrine and can see through walls. I talk to a woman who says in five years, anyone will be able to cook up designer drugs in their house with something like those pod coffee makers, except twice as expensive. I don't believe her, but then remember a time back in 1988 when an Ameritech installation guy told me to invest in wireless communication stock, because within a dozen or so years nobody would have land lines anymore. I laughed, didn't believe him, and do the same to this woman.

An hour later, I'm scouring Brookline for a place with decent hot dogs, and suddenly remember the thousands of dead rats I'm going to have in my room when I get back to the hotel. I'm concerned about the shit and piss they probably left everywhere in their death throes, but think maybe I can make a themed web page and get back the money in ad revenue.

I run into a guy who looks like Jimi Hendrix at age seventy, running a hot dog that actually grills the dogs instead of boiling them, and I blow through a hundred bucks of cased meat while he tells me a story about how after the release of the *Perverse* album, Jesus Jones took an extended hiatus because four of the members were addicted to Chicken McNuggets.

* * *

A new mumblecore movie comes out that has a sex scene between Lena Dunham and Jonah Hill, and it shows full penetration. I buy a ticket for a midnight screening as a goof, so I can post about it on Facebook ironically. (I'm stupid like that — I actually paid money to see the band Creed once.) The movie is only playing in this popup screening room in Brooklyn that also

3-D prints steampunk vegan cupcakes at a food truck outside. I don't have a mustache, so they won't let me in.

After walking for a few hours in the dark, I find a 24-hour sushi restaurant that has the dim sum conveyor belt system running to each table, with little plates and tins continually rotating around the dining room. A waiter with no eyebrows, strung out on methadone, comes over to my table, gives me a glass of warm Tang, and asks me for my family medical history. I proceed to rattle off all 272,000 words of *The Personal Memoirs of Ulysses S. Grant*, replacing the word "Grant" with "Konrath." (It's a trick I learned in college, for boring first dates.)

The waiter says, "We have Pepsi, no Coke," and vanishes. I'm the only person in the dining room. The conveyor belts grumble to life, the belts propelling a stream of round metal tins and bamboo baskets. I open a basket and it contains a Reese's peanut butter cup on top of a pile of maggots. After that, there's a tray with a human eyeball packed in a layer of shredded beets. I know the next one is going to have olives in it and it will make me puke, so I leave, without paying for the Tang. In six months, they will send my check to a collection agency, who end up chasing me for $863 in fees and interest.

* * *

My coworker Todd from the paint factory brings a box of Taco Bell burritos to the funeral service. Henry Kissinger died, and everyone at the plant is invited, because he was a big fan of our semi-gloss interior paint.

"I'm not taking any chances with that foreign food," Todd says. "I know my 'Bell is cooked to exacting standards." He would die six months later of Hepatitis A he caught when a fry cook took a dump in the refried bean vat. His family tried to sue Yum! Foods, but there's fine print at the bottom of the hot sauce packets that releases liability for this.

I leave the reception and drive to a Showbiz Pizza place by the Amtrak station, where the train conductors go to bet on skee-ball. Kissinger is there, playing *Q\*Bert*. I tell him I was just at his funeral, and without looking up from the game, he says, "Fuckin' taxes, man."

* * *

I'm flying to Midway to see Andy Kaufman talk at a necrophilia conference. (He's somehow still alive, and was just in hiding for thirty-something years.) The Boeing 767 loses both engines, total catastrophic failure. The pilot gets on the PA and is freaking out, saying we have to make a water landing on Lake Michigan, and the plane doesn't have any life preservers because this model of plane got rid of them all so they could carry more twenty-dollar snack trays.

I very clearly have the "well, this is how I die" thing running through my head, start re-playing every regret in my life, also mixed with a desire to talk to a woman in row 18 who looks like someone I went on two dates with in 2002 and I thought it was going great until she told me she had a husband and was a lesbian. I duck and cover, and think about Ethiopian Airlines

Flight 961, which crashed in the water of the Indian Ocean like a hundred yards from the shore, and everyone drowned because they popped their inflatable vests while still inside the plane and couldn't get through the exit hatches.

Oddly enough, the water landing goes fine, just as smooth as a regular ground landing, and the airport has a bunch of water taxis waiting to take us to shore. It's actually even faster than a regular landing, because we get to skip security and don't have to wait for a gate. Everyone is given their bags, and they're drenched with lake water. I think I lose a Krokus cassette in the scuffle, and I never got my snack plate, but I'm otherwise okay.

As we walk through the concourse, I see my lawyer and buddy Lars, handcuffed and sitting on a fake plastic tree planter, surrounded by mall cops. I ask him if he was on the plane with me, and he says he wasn't; he just heard about it on WGN and drove to the airport because plane crashes were a great place to cruise for pussy. But the mall cops were trying to arrest him on some trumped up charge, like "intent to resist arrest and attempt of assault with a non-deadly weapon on a non-commissioned TSA seasonal temp officer" because he pissed on a vending machine. It was a USA Today newspaper machine, and they were trying to get an FBI officer to add a federal wiretapping charge or something.

"You should go find the CNN crew," he tells me. "They're not broadcasting on a ten-second delay. You could totally pull out your cock on live TV." I think maybe it would be a good time to talk to that woman from 18A about getting a drink, but I can't find her, and the airline starts giving me shit about charging me twice for my luggage because of the added weight from the lake water.

* * *

I listen to an old Steve Martin tape in my car stereo and cruise up and down arterial streets, looking for the location where a prominent amateur income tax enthusiast was shot back in 1974. I only have a crayon sketch of a map from the guy's long-lost uncle, who is now in an insane asylum for hearing voices and digging holes in his back yard without a building permit. (Never buy a house with a Homeowners' Association — zoning is ridiculous.)

His directions make no sense, and Google isn't helping. Then again, I have a horrible sense of direction. In my pre-GPS days back in New York, I must have walked an extra hundred miles a year, getting off a subway and heading east instead of west, not realizing it until I hit the edge of the island and had to turn around. Landmarks in any city larger than a million people look the same to me, and it only gets worse as I get older and they keep plopping down identical three-story apartment buildings complexes that always, always have a Subway restaurant or a dry cleaner that closes at four PM on the bottom floor.

Must have given up... now at a French restaurant... not the fancy kind with frog's legs and ten-course meals, but the bistro kind, with baguette sandwiches and stale pastries. I'm thinking about a Douglas MacArthur tribute band I once saw in the basement of a gay bar in Bunker Hill. I was wearing a Batman costume for some reason, or at least the rubber mask. The lead singer smoked a corn cob pipe, but kept stopping every song so he could clean the grease from his sunglasses. His skin was unnaturally oily, and during one of the breaks, the bass player kept a walking bass line going while the singer went on an extended soliloquy about how he wanted to try Proactiv face cream, but he hated their sponsor Adam Levine. He said he tried to get on that singing competition once, doing a cover of a Suzanna Vega song (not sure which, probably "My Name is Luca") when Levine got out a gong and started ringing it to banish him from the show. This was all on the untelevised first round, so there's no footage of it — trust me, I've looked. It's a horrible wormhole to fall down.

Nothing in the restaurant looks edible. I drink an Orangina soda, which I hate, and look at my phone to find a co-working space or internet cafe or some other place I can crash and work for a few hours without having to continually buy more food that I would shove in my fat face, regardless of quality. This was the dead era after the internet cafe fad had passed and before the co-working fad had fully developed, so I can't find anything practical, aside from sitting in my car in a mall parking lot. I try this, seat reclined, windows fogging up, and fall asleep in minutes.

* * *

In a restaurant named Corn Dog Day Afternoon — it's in the basement of a building that houses a ground-floor PetSmart, and ten stories of office space used by discount law firms and yoga studios. The restaurant is made to look like a Brooklyn bank from the Seventies, just like the Al Pacino movie. Above the register is a black-and-white head shot of John Cazale that is so faded, it looks green. The picture is autographed, but looks like it was done with a rubber stamp.

The restaurant owner is obsessed with asphyxiation. Glass display cases on the walls contain an extensive collection of pieces of food that patrons had choked on and then had heimlich'ed back out. Above the cash register, affixed to a wooden plaque, there is a faded, lacquered foot-long kielbasa that Norman Rockwell had allegedly eaten whole and vomited back up.

The cashier asks me if I've heard about the homosexual subtext of *The Deer Hunter*. I only remember the Russian roulette thing, and I really want a corn dog, so I say, "Sure, whatever" and try to order food. He keeps talking for twenty minutes, and the smell of the french fries is unbearable. I finally leave, go to an imitation Subway restaurant, and eat an entire pound of warm spiral-cut ham, which isn't as good as it sounds.

* * *

I find a signature Richard Nixon bowling ball in an ex-girlfriend's apartment. She subleased a two-bedroom duplex made out of the back half of an iron lung factory built in 1886. It had a one-car garage that could barely hold a Yugo, maybe converted out of a horse stable. It inexplicably has the bowling ball in it, rolling loose on the concrete floor, no bag or case.

The finger holes look like they are drilled for a Slender Man monster, spaced nearly a foot apart. Nothing special about the finish — no swirls or glitter metallic, just plain old black, covered in scratches, Big Dick's signature auto-penned onto the surface below the company logo. Heavy, too — I think it's a sixteen-pounder, but I can't find a scale to confirm. I bring it to a pawn shop to see if it's worth any money, and they say it's against the Geneva Convention to buy or sell anything Richard Nixon-related, because it's technically a war crime trophy.

I spend months trying to find a way to destroy the ball: fireworks, shotgun blasts, homemade acid. A gas chainsaw doesn't do anything, and then I break the chain and almost kill myself. One of my neighbors suggests bringing it to a fortune-teller to cast a spell on it, and I consider beating him to death with the ball, but I can't get a good grip with those wide finger-holes.

\* \* \*

I'm getting ten teeth drilled by a fat dentist who looks like Mike Ditka with a bad comb-over. He's eating a sausage and pepper sandwich as he's working. The dude has an obsession with *Maxim* magazine and won't shut up about it. He's telling me about how John Wayne Gacy wrote a western novel back when he was on death row and they were serializing it. "It's no Cormac McCarthy, but what the hell. Look how much his paintings are going for on eBay."

The drilling smells like rancid Salisbury steak, and it's mixing with the smell of the juicy sausage sandwich and has me on the verge of stream-vomiting everywhere. The odor reminds me of the time right out of college when I found a Safeway coupon for Swanson beef pot pies for three for a dollar, and each box had a mail-in coupon for fifty cents cash back, so I bought $200 of pot pies and got $300 back. The only problem was I had to eat pot pies made of borderline inedible meat for months. And you can't microwave pot pies, so my house was always like three hundred degrees from baking the things. (I think there was a Tom Hanks movie about this.)

I walk home after a few more hours of drilling. I'm bleeding profusely, my mouth stuffed with gauze, and my jaw muscles are absolutely destroyed. In the parking lot of a used car dealer, some kind of weird radio station on-location promo deal is going on, with a guy dressed as a giant clam. A bunch of freaks wearing day-glow yellow painter's overalls are dancing like one of those goofy Intel commercials, and people are honking their car horns rhythmically. The overalls people are handing out helium balloons to passers-by, who are inhaling them and then passing out on the sidewalk. One of the guys offers me a balloon and says, "SPOILER ALERT – ROSEBUD IS THE SLED!"

\* \* \*

The EPA is suing my grandfather. His estate, rather — a year after he died, probate court found a new will that specified that his money should be used to build a robotic, fire-breathing tyrannosaurus rex next to his grave. I thought they should sell tickets, but he was buried in Denali National Park, at the site where that Christopher McCandless *Into the Wild* kid died. It takes about three days to hike to his grave on foot, and there's no way to drive there. I did the trip once on an ATV, but the bathroom situation of long-range hikes doesn't appeal to me.

I read all the EPA paperwork while I'm visiting my dad's house in Rochester, New York. I think it's Christmas, or another holiday break. I also find a shelf of mementos and old books of mine that I'd left behind at my parents' house at some point, model railroad magazines and report cards. There's a court summons from 1994, with the return address of "The So-Called Income Tax Board of Monroe County." I remember getting in an argument with the county over sentient lawn mowers, but I'd skipped town before the warrant for my arrest showed up. I paid a pre-trial diversion agreement, and used it as an excuse to get out of jury duty for the next decade. I consider scanning the old papers, digital hoarding, but then my uncle shows up, wants me to explain why I'm against requiring everyone getting the ten commandments tattooed on their thigh.

I don't know anyone in Rochester except a guy who did performance art involving eating broken pyrex beakers and screaming into a tape recorder about how the band Bachman-

Turner Overdrive was a fake front for the Canadian Security Intelligence Service. And there's an ex-girlfriend from years ago, who I think had four kids since high school. I meet with her at the Irondequoit Mall at the half-ass food court with no real food. She works in a Hallmark store, and tells me the kid thing was a Facebook ruse to get rid of a stalker.

I go back to her house because I don't want to stay in my family's basement anymore — it has a termite problem and I keep waking up in the middle of the night covered in bugs. We start having sex on a water softener next to the washer and dryer, but after a few minutes, she finds an old electric typewriter and decides to start applying to art schools. I tell her I know a place I can get her free photocopies, but when I drive her to the strip mall, the copy joint has been turned into a falafel restaurant, run by a Sikh guy with a giant sword. I offer to buy her some hummus or something, but she says she can't eat anything with vegetables in it.

We go across the street to a Miami Grill restaurant and order a hundred roast beef sandwiches with no buns and a bottle of champagne, for old times' sake. She tells me she got really involved in astronomy back in the early 2000s, and almost married a professional go-kart driver, but he lost all his money in a *Magic: The Gathering* pyramid scheme and jumped off a bridge. I go to the bathroom, and while I'm doing my business at a urinal, an old lady worker came in and dumps fifty pounds of rotten gyro meat in the urinal next to me. By the time I finish and wash my hands thoroughly, the ex-girlfriend is gone, and my food is missing.

\* \* \*

There are alien egg pods at the A&P deli counter, like the HR Giger artwork. "Jesus died to make America great," says the fat butcher, slicing the pods into thin slices, like a salami. He says he used to fly choppers back in 'Nam, and knows what he's talking about. He can obviously run a Hobart, but I don't know if I'd trust him with a Huey.

"Sun gods will destroy this planet, unless we learn to self-medicate," he says. "It's happened before — it'll happen again. Second law of thermodynamics. It's all going down, so fuck and steal what you can. Party on, Garth." He slides the wax paper-wrapped package across the counter, and I pick it up and drop it into my cart. I don't even know why I'm buying them, and will probably just put them in the fridge for six months and then throw them in the garbage.

When I get to the cashier up front, everyone is crying because the inventor of Necco Wafers has been shot in the head JFK-style while driving around Texas in a convertible limo. The New England Confectionery Company is a family-owned business, and nobody knows if the owner will survive. I think about hoarding as many rolls of the candy as possible, because I actually like them, but when I look in the candy bins by the cash registers, they only have the all-chocolate rolls, which is bullshit.

* * *

I wake up in my buddy's bathtub in Salt Lake City, Utah. There's a fierce snowstorm outside that's been blowing all night, slamming powder against the windows like a hurricane. The house is covered in a thick blanket of white, and I can barely open the front door because of a waist-high snowdrift. The Winter Olympics rented a snow machine from an indoor ski place in Dubai, and when they turned it on in the frozen weather, it was like that one Kurt Vonnegut book where the whole world froze over from ice-nine, instant snow everywhere.

The bathtub smells like lime deposits, which isn't a bad smell, but lime has that weird property where it's both fresh and dirty, like white sand or *Playboy* magazine. I take a whore bath in the tub, rinsing the pits and crotch as much as possible. When I get out, my friend has used a pair of samurai swords to chop an ice tunnel to my car. The streets are plowed, and it looks like a 3-D version of *Pac Man*, white walls of ice on either side of the road. I need breakfast, but the only shops on the outskirts of town are tattoo parlors and *Total Recall*-style memory implant vacation joints.

My day job is selling the computer-controlled machines used at public executions to inject lethal chemicals into death row inmates. They are an add-on to old IBM PCs still running OS/2. While driving across Utah, I make cold calls with a headset like a McDonald's drive-through employee. I was talking to a guy in China, and we somehow get into a conversation about Magic 8-Balls. He has no idea how they work or where they get the answers, or why someone would use one, and I'm trying to explain it to him, with no success. Every time I say, "It's just a stupid game for kids," he pauses for like sixty seconds and then says, "well how does it know answers?"

South of Provo, I pull into a gas station with a Mexican restaurant, which doesn't have chimichangas, but does make a passable enchilada. (The enchilada is the poor man's chimichanga; a sure sign of a restaurant without a proper deep fryer.) I'm eating a plate of six cheese enchiladas, and a guy in a sombrero with a ukulele runs in and says Lake Utah smells like jizz. I pay him twenty dollars to not play the ukulele while I'm trying to eat. He gets mad and tells me to move to North Dakota. I tell him I was born in North Dakota, then realize that doesn't help my argument. He takes my twenty dollars, and plays ukulele anyway.

The ukulele dude plays "When You Wish Upon a Star" and I want to ask him why every damn ukulele player has to do that song, but I burn the roof of my mouth on enchilada sauce and can't talk. I go back to driving, and after about an hour, I'm outside Toronto, which makes no sense, but I start listening to the first Rush album anyway, in case I get pulled over by a cop and I have to prove I'm Canadian.

\* \* \*

I watch an old grainy, snowy VHS tape of a Captain Beefheart late night talk show, from maybe the mid-Eighties, when everyone had a talk show. He would interview people, like any other talk show, but go off on bizarre tangents, totally ignoring the guest, never getting back on track. It's so chaotic and unnerving, it is pure art.

For example, Chevy Chase was on the show, and Beefheart was trying to convince him that the movie *Fletch* was really about alien abductions. And Chevy was like, no, really, it's about this newspaper reporter who... "IT'S ABOUT ALIENS, I'VE SEEN THEM!" Then he opens up a curtain on stage left, and he's got a giant UFO set, and he forces Chase to climb up on it while he's screaming about how Fletch Fletcher is a reptilian.

Chevy Chase reluctantly climbs the UFO, and acts goofy, but you can tell he is scared shitless. He falls off the top of the UFO, and at first you think it's going to be a pratfall like he usually does, but he lands hands-first, violently, compound fractures of his wrists, bones sticking out, blood gushing everywhere.

As they cut to commercial, Beefheart is still screaming, "IT'S LIKE THAT TWILIGHT ZONE EPISODE WHERE THE GUY HAS THREE HANDS!"

* * *

I'm eating a box of club crackers on my front porch and watching a guy across the street try to wrap bologna around his alcohol-monitoring ankle bracelet. He looks like Flavor Flav, but he has a barometer on a chain on his chest instead of a clock. I cross the street to talk to him, and a production assistant blocks me, asks me to sign a waiver, because they're filming the whole thing for a reality show. I refuse to sign anything, and go back to the other side of the street to watch the activity unfold.

A column of Chinese battle tanks roll down the wide avenue. A dissident from Beijing, carrying two plastic bags full of hard candy, walks in front of the lead tank, and forces it to stop. It tries to turn, and he jumps in front of it again. After three or more iterations of this, the dissident yells, "STOP, HAMMERTIME!" and throws the candy into the crowd, then starts breakdancing on the asphalt, doing the worm, a head spin, and several other maneuvers. Finally, the front Type 59 tank guns it, plows over the man, and continues down the road.

Sirens start in the distance, cop cars and fire trucks fast approaching. I walk to a nearby Domino's pizza, and talk to the manager, who looks like Weird Al Yankovich circa 1989. He convinces me that within five years, all take-out pizzas will be made from human flesh and recycled medical waste. "I've known at least twenty people who have had a section of their colon removed. That stuff has to go somewhere. Domino's Pizza is people! And we're so cost-engineered in here, they're talking about eliminating the boxes. When you order a pizza, you'll have to bring in your own cloth bag, or carry the pie home in your hands. They're not even going to include sauce anymore, extra charge."

"Can't you just eat it right here in the store?" I ask.

"We don't have the permits for that. And you get more than three, four people in this little closet of a store, and it's a war zone. They tried it in an experimental store in Kansas once. The place got burned to the fucking ground within a week."

"You know anything about the Chinese tanks outside?"

"Something about copyright law. Or maybe it's net neutrality. I don't keep up with this shit anymore. My brother lost a thousand dollars trying to buy an internet. I'll keep using the regular telephone. I've got a bank of ten phones in the back room. Why change?"

\* \* \*

I'm working at a suit company. It's a low-rent rip-off of Men's Wearhouse, and even has a bearded owner/spokesman who looks like Al Zimmer. All the suits smell of mothballs and flameproof nylon, like cheap camping tents you'd buy at Kmart. We mostly get business from the state prison, when they need to bury someone in dress clothes after they are executed.

The job only pays six bucks an hour, and it involves a lot of ironing and folding, which I cannot deal with. But the owner's son, who is like the second-in-command, never shows up for work. He's really into the import tuner car scene, and he gets pinched on conversion or reckless driving charges like every other week. He's been stealing vehicles for years, parting them out and telling people the pieces are from one of Paul Walker's cars.

The owner calls me in for a meeting and tells me I can enter a probationary managerial position and eventually take over the company when he dies. But he warns me that he takes a lot of vitamins. Also, I have to start calling people who wrote bad checks and get them to pay up. I think this could make a good sitcom treatment, but then I realize it was probably already a *Murphy Brown* episode.

\* \* \*

We're driving an ice cream truck in rural Montana, and I'm shoveling charcoal out the back window. My buddy Irwin is driving the right-hand-drive AMC, throttle wide open, and we're going maybe 40. I'm standing thigh-deep in dusty briquettes, wondering if we robbed a Kingsford factory, and there's maybe two tons of the stuff in the back of the squat little van. I feel like if I unload all the charcoal, we might be able to hit 55.

We get pulled over by a motorcycle cop, and I stop the shoveling while Irwin talks to him. I pop open a Big K cola and chug half the can, but my face and arms are covered in coal like I'm a chimney sweep in a Dickens novel, and I estimate I drink a briquette worth of dust. Isn't charcoal a new health fad, though? Or is that just skin care? Irwin tells the cop that we are driving to Montana because of that Frank Zappa song, and the officer explains that you can't really farm dental floss. He lets us go with a warning, and tells us to try the land crab.

We're somehow in Minnesota, driving on the I-90 corridor, and I have an overwhelming urge to stop at a mall and buy a cellular phone. I'm done with the shoveling, and trying to wipe myself clean with a single wet-nap from Kentucky Fried Chicken.

"I don't see why they don't put more KFCs in gas stations," Irwin said. "Hell, the Colonel started KFC in the back of a gas station. What comes around goes around."

We go to this mall that's absolutely dead, and I scrub off the rest of the coal dust in the men's room, but destroy five sinks and my shirt in the process. In a Sam Goody or FYE or one of those corporate music stores, I buy a Winger shirt for thirty dollars, because I have to wear something. Irwin goes through all the used tapes, because we've been listening to the same Credence greatest hits tape for days. He finds a Pearl Jam album that has Eddie Vedder's voice digitally removed and replaced with Danny Bonaduce telling stupid jokes over the rest of the band. It's honestly a good idea. I also get a box of pretzel bites, but the cheese dip is rancid and I end up throwing out the whole thing before we get to the parking lot.

* * *

I'm driving around town with a Korean computer science major, trying to find someone that has the 188-minute version of the 1978 *Superman* movie that was edited for TV with like an hour of extra junk in it. I need it for a telecommunications midterm exam. He's driving an old Hyundai Sonata from the early Nineties, done up like the General Lee, bright orange with the 01 on the door and the words "General Lee" done in the Korean Hangul alphabet, and the roof has a North Korean flag on it.

We weave through traffic, at a top speed of about seventeen miles an hour, as the tiny engine sounds like it's about to explode. He tells me he lost 200 pounds eating nothing but potatoes for a year, and watching four hours of pornography a day. I don't know if that's a North Korean thing, or a new fad diet.

"*Bust a Nut 24* is a good movie," he tells me. He's gone deep into a k-hole about studio-shot pornography, like I care. "Excellent cinematography. I think it was filmed in Vista-Vision widescreen. Just like *Star Wars*. I can loan you a copy on Super VHS."

"No thanks, I never saw the first 23." I say.

He pulls into the parking lot of a Roy Rogers fried chicken shop, clutches his chest. Massive coronary, fatal heart attack, 144% blockage of the widow-maker. I guess that potato diet was bullshit, but I will forever think it had something to do with me saying I wouldn't watch his favorite porno. At least he pulled over and put the car in park first. It takes me ten minutes to get out, though — he welded his doors shut.

\* \* \*

I'm in a Fred Meyer in Alaska, looking at the bear spray products. Alex Jones is in the lawn chair department, wearing full ninja gear, swinging around a pair of katana swords, screaming about the Hobbit movies. The store intercom is blasting an Enya greatest hits album, which probably triggered him. His face is redder than a can of Coke, and I'm certain he's going to stroke out in thirty seconds. On closer inspection, he's actually using wooden training swords, but I don't want to end up in the crossfire of a suicide-by-cop, so I rush to the cashier to pay for a set of universal-fit bucket seat covers and a ten-pound box of frozen taquitos.

Days later, I'm at a colonoscopy booth in a mall, and the prep nurse tells me they can't do the procedure because I ate the frozen taquitos the morning of the exam, and their scope isn't insured for that. The nurse smells like cocktail onions, and it makes me want a hot dog loaded with everything. I tell her it took me months to get the insurance authorization and day off of work, and I need to get the test done now. She counter-offers and says she can give me the drugs, but no test.

I sit in the parking lot of the Macy's, holding an IV bag of Demerol and valium, the tube of precious liquids threaded into my arm. A group of old women in walkers and scooters are protesting people who don't cook steaks well done. They have posters of medium-rare steaks with captions like "RARE MEAT IS MURDER" and "GOD HATES BLOOD." I think about how hard it would be to install rudder pedals in my car to play a flight simulator game while I'm stuck in traffic.

A Latvian guy with a food cart knocks on my windows, scares the shit out of me. He's got a push cart, like the people who sell shaved ice, but it's full of frozen fudge. I ask him if he's got a microwave or something, because I don't want to eat frozen fudge and chip a tooth. He starts laughing and calls me a pussy.

\* \* \*

The IRS cloned Abraham Lincoln, and booked appearances at various pro wrestling events so people would like the new simplified tax form, which is really like twice as difficult as a 1040-EZ and designed to make people lose money. At a BuffaLouie's bar and grill, I watch a pay-per-view simulcast from Columbus, Ohio where Randy Orton accidentally breaks Lincoln's neck during a promo. The replays of it saturate social media for months. Someone takes the LiveLeak raw footage of Honest Abe's vertebrae being smashed into dust with a steel chair, and dubs "Yakety Saks" over it. I think it gets a million hits, and is on *Talk Soup*.

\* \* \*

I'm watching college basketball in a gas station that mostly sells stuff to smoke crack and huff paint. (Chore Boy steel wool, white socks, little roses in a glass tube, etc.) I think I have a small wager on the Arkansas Razorbacks, but I don't remember if it's a fantasy baseball thing or just straight-up betting on the spread. The announcer is talking about how he got jumped after a St. Louis minor league soccer game. The muggers took him to the Gateway Arch and forced him at gunpoint to ride up and down the arch in that goofy sideways elevator. Some sexual thing, I guess. Didn't even take his wallet or press pass.

An Indian guy behind the counter at the gas station is yelling at someone on the phone about a broken Seagate hard drive.

He's talking in Hindi, which I don't understand, but he keeps saying "Seagate Barracuda" in English, so that's my guess.

It's the bottom of the fourth, and the Arkansas pitcher is melting down, has walked fourteen batters in a row. The catcher comes to the mound between batters and punches the pitcher in the nuts. The other team (Texas A&M) starts bunting for no reason, I think just to be dicks. I give up on the game and leave.

The insect infestation is still going on outside, and I contemplate buying a large fog machine, or maybe a coal-fired locomotive that could burn green logs to produce massive clouds of smoke. I tried bug dope, 100% DDT, and it did nothing but make me hallucinate. I can't sleep, have built up an unholy tolerance to Benadryl. I could eat an entire bottle and still fly a plane. I am asleep, in the dream, but I really need sleep.

* * *

A famous author of children's books on communism and welding died in a hydrogen-powered taxicab explosion. Everyone is posting pictures of his artwork carved into their arms, quotes from his books burned into their faces and foreheads. A girl I went to high school with hires an Uber and tells the driver to go to an address in the middle of the ocean, hoping he will drive into the sea and drown them. (She saw it on an episode of *The Office*. It doesn't work, but probably could.)

I'm ignoring all of this. For some stupid reason, I'm trying to find a tax law site with information on Japanese radial engines from World War II. It's to win an argument with my buddy who's stuck in Yugoslavia with the army. I didn't even think Yugoslavia existed anymore, but he spends six hours a day scrolling through Reddit and shitposting *Touched by an Angel* memes.

Someone leaves a can of creamed corn on my doorstep, with a note that says "I KNOW YOU READ AND ENJOYED HIS BOOKS IN THE FIFTH GRADE YOU FUCKING LIAR." I didn't even read children's books when I was a child. I deactivate my Facebook account, but then reactivate it twenty minutes later out of boredom.

\* \* \*

A guy from the Major League Baseball Authentication Program keeps calling my cell phone, five or ten times an hour. The first time I answer, he wants me to sign a paper swearing that Keith Hernandez bought my George Foreman grill in 2002. I tell him to send over whatever — I vaguely remember somebody buying the piece of shit grill in Astoria, Queens at a yard sale I was holding on the sidewalk in the front of my building so I could buy tickets to see a Styx tribute band. Maybe it was him, I don't know. A lot of guys in Queens look like Keith Hernandez.

A courier shows up at my apartment with a sword, tells me he has to cut open my finger so I can sign the paperwork in blood. Something has happened to my left hand — the skin has the texture and color of a rubber Stretch Armstrong doll from the Seventies. I wonder if the guy cut me with his sword, if I would leak corn starch instead of blood, like the gel-filled Kenner toy. I also start thinking about wearing a glove of some sort, but this is right after Michael Jackson died, and I don't want people to think it's some sort of tribute. I tell the courier to go screw, and the phone calls continue.

I go to work — I'm washing dishes at a Hooters restaurant inside Grand Central Station. The comedian Kevin Nealon is working there, researching a part for a movie. He spends most of the day eating food from plates sent back to the kitchen, and reminding me not to tell anyone he's a famous actor. I go to the front of house to get more salt shakers to wash. There's a large stone fireplace in the dining room, partly for ambience, but the owner's son also uses it to cook meth. I consider putting my head in the fireplace and doing it up Sylvia Plath style, but it's too smoky and smells like burning plastic.

I see a guy from high school who played about two minutes of football in college for some dumb state school that later got the NCAA death penalty for recruiting violations. He's covered in wing sauce and sexually harassing the waitresses. He's got a flat top and looks like an out-of-shape retired NFL player, except he probably sells insurance or works for his dad and makes ten times as much money as me. I tell Kevin Nealon about it, and we both jerk off in a jar of secret sauce and bring him out a batch of dishwasher's special recipe wings, extra salty.

After we close out the place, we walk to a 24-hour steak buffet joint and buy all the Mexican dishwashers a round of shots. We all start yelling "¡Matando Güeros!" and throwing shot glasses at the passing traffic. My hand has somehow healed back to normal — maybe from the hot dishwater — but now I'm worried because Nealon keeps trying to get me to go play golf with him the next day, and he's got a six AM tee time. I tell him I'm afraid the hand is going to revert back, and I need to sleep. He calls me an asshole, but pays the bar tab anyway.

* * *

I'm at a garage sale, and I realize every item sitting on the tables in the driveway of this house are body pieces that Ed Gein cut apart and cured in a hot house. I go to ask the owner if any of the stuff is real, and he's sitting on a toilet he's installed in the middle of the garage, bolted to the drain in the middle of the floor. "I've got IBS. It's a legitimate medical condition. Are you here about the hearse? Keys are on the table."

I grab the keys — they are on a ZZ Top keychain, like the video — and go behind the house. There's an old Cadillac hearse, one of the shitty models from the Eighties when GM was fucking everything up, a giant boat with a V-6 engine in it that could barely hit highway speed. I start the car, but it has six accelerator pedals, all next to each other, and I wonder if big bomber airplanes with six engines are set up like this. I start driving, smashing different pedals randomly, each making a different engine noise but having little effect on the overall speed of the car.

When I press the cruise control, it takes over steering the vehicle, so I crawl into the back of the hearse and start watching a movie on the big projector screen TV above the coffin area. It's playing *Bridget Jones's Diary*, which is a weird coincidence because back in late 2001, I tried starting a rumor in that Osama bin Ladin was obsessed with that movie, and then years later when they killed him, it turns out he had like six dozen copies of it at his house.

I can't stand the movie, so I open the back hatch and try to push the coffin onto the road behind me. The coffin is locked down to the bed of the hearse somehow, and when I open it, it's filled with rotting Go-Gurt containers. I disengage the autopilot cruise control, and leave the car in the parking lot of a mall that still has a Montgomery Ward department store.

* * *

Geddy Lee keeps crank calling my parents' house, pretending to be an effeminate insurance salesman, and I can't get him to stop. This is right before Caller ID became a thing, and I wonder if maybe I can build a Caller ID box with a bunch of junk from the computer store. He eventually gets bored of the pranks, but still phones me from every city while he's on tour. He's trying to eat at every McDonald's in the world, and reports in on each location, always complaining that they never have poutine like they do in Quebec.

* * *

A guy in McDonald's has a cutoff grinder plugged into the wall, and he's chopping apart an IBM XT computer case, so it will fit a modern motherboard and play *Minecraft*. A fountain of blue sparks shoots across the dining room in a wide arc, lighting the garbage on the floor on fire. He's got an apple pie hanging from his mouth like a Cuban bandito clenching a cigar in his teeth. It is 10:31 and the McDonald's doesn't have either breakfast or lunch items, just pies and boxes of cookies. The Diet Coke is also out of syrup, dispensing a light brown water with very little fizz. I buy a box of cookies and a bottle of water, and give up on any hope of a meal until later.

I go to a JC Penney photo studio for work — they want corporate photos for the web site. I haven't shaved in a week, and look like a serial killer. I stop in the public restroom next to the JC Penney hair salon full of old ladies getting their hair re-blued. The bathroom is done up in groovy earth-tone tiles from 1974, and has a semi-circular trough sink that looks like it was stolen from a Montessori school. I throw up in the sink a few times — photo anxiety — then wash my face with pink liquid soap, and wander the mall for a few minutes to get my head back on.

I find a corridor in the mall filled with bankrupt, vacated stores that have been converted into Ethiopian restaurants and/ or shooting ranges. I'm still starving, but I know I shouldn't eat Ethiopian food on an empty stomach. I go to a gun range that used to be a Camelot Records and think about shooting a few hundred rounds on an AK-47, but the kid running it says I need to buy a membership card for fifty bucks, and I have to take a hundred-question blue book essay test on the history of the

*Tonight Show* with Johnny Carson, and if I write anything about Jay Leno, it's an automatic disqualification. I agree with this policy, but I don't have time for this nonsense.

\* \* \*

I'm at a brewpub in an old corrugated steel factory that used to be used to make malathion gas. The bar is really popular because it has three-dollar pints on Tuesdays and no mosquitos. I read the back of the menu, which has an article about how the place was used by Dow or Monsanto or something to do chemical research for the Manhattan Project during the war. I'd leave, but there's no other place to get food for miles. I order a really good deep-dish pizza by the slice called The Colon Blow. They also have a Tetris machine, and someone entered "FUK" for all the top ten scores.

\* \* \*

I'm watching two guys in sparkle-orange motorcycle helmets take turns beating each other in the head with a pool cue. Guy one smacks guy two in the helmet, much laughter, then he hands over the stick and the other guy reciprocates. I don't know if it's a twisted version of a traditional duel, or a mating ritual. It's strange behavior for the parking lot of a bread store. And I don't know why I'm buying ten loaves of Italian bread in the middle of the week.

An old lady with a grandma wire shopping basket pushes past me, says something about fighting in Normandy. I want to ask her to repeat it, but I don't care, and I've lost my voice. It's not clear if I'm sick, or I can't hear myself talking because the wiring is patched together wrong, like when you dial into an online conference with a broken headset.

I go to Petco to buy a talking bird that I can use as an interpreter. An old lady who does bird rescue is trying to talk me into buying a thousand-dollar parrot, but then I remember they could live to be like a hundred years old, or at least old enough to long outlive me. On the flip side, the first time my landlord doesn't turn on the heat in my building until it is well below zero for months, the bird would probably die, or catch some kind of bird pneumonia that would cost me tens of thousands of dollars in vet bills. I can't deal with any of this, cannot have this responsibility hanging over my head, so I walk next door to Nobody Beats the Wiz and buy a PlayStation.

\* \* \*

I can't remember the details of the dream — something about wandering around a cave that looks like part of the *Myst* video game. What I do remember is that I'm narrating my every movement in the dream, and writing down the narration. Then I stop every sentence or two, edit the narration, check the verb tense, wordsmith the text to make it flow better. I wake up and realize I've been editing this book for too fucking long.

* * *

They've invented a new color, something deeper than an indigo or violet, but not quite black. They're calling it Zixufgo. I don't know if *invented* is the right word, I think they reallocated part of the light spectrum. It's like how they reallocated all the old analog TV channels and auctioned off that part of the spectrum, so Verizon and AT&T could dump their high-speed wireless signals there.

The whole thing with the new color is designed to sell more TVs. You can't see the new color on an old TV or computer. It's confusing because news articles try to describe the color, but pretty much every journalist has been fired in the last decade, so the descriptions are all written by the same borderline illiterate copy editor, and make no sense.

I go to a TV store and look at the color, and cannot tell the god damned difference. It looks like dark purple to me. Maybe I'm zixufgo-blind. Maybe they'll make a medication for that, and every doctor I see for the rest of my life will force a prescription on me, even though it makes me shit blood and shoot pus from my eye sockets twenty-four hours a day.

Somebody already registered Zixufgo.com and pointed it to a porn site. And it isn't even pornography that contained the color Zixufgo in it, which seems like it would be a slam dunk. It's just a page of boring clips hosted on other porn sites, plus tons of pop-up ads.

A week later, every Zixufgo-compatible smart TV gets a virus that melts the picture element and fills the room with poison gas. There's a class-action lawsuit, and ten years later, anyone who files the right paperwork (it requires a lawyer) can get a check for $7.68.

\* \* \*

Eating a potato salad sandwich and watching two backhoe operators dig rows and columns of shallow graves in a vacant lot. I'm in the parking lot of a church that's selling ethnic picnic food and illegal scratch-off tickets. I buy a five-dollar ticket and win a Kodak Tele-Ektra 300 film camera from the mid-Seventies, which is completely useless because it shoots 110 cartridge film, now impossible to find or develop. But it is in a nice box, and the camera itself is branded for the movie *Deep Throat*, with a picture of Linda Lovelace silkscreened on the bottom.

I gorge down so much potato salad, I have to take a cab to the emergency room and get my stomach pumped. My doctor is a twelve-year-old kid with a medical degree and an attitude problem. He tells me I need to stop eating fiber and start antiquing on the weekend. I don't know if he means I am supposed to drive around Connecticut looking for antiques to buy, or apply various acids and solvents to furniture to make them look older. The hospital is inside a Circuit City, so I buy a new DVD player and a box of floppy discs on the way out.

* * *

Locked in an old furniture factory, and it's freezing, snowing outside, but the interior of the old building is maybe 40 or 50 degrees. The furniture manufacturer has been gone for decades; they now rent the space to a conglomerate, as a storage facility. It's full of boxes of knock-off GI Joe dolls that have defective kung fu grips that would take out an eye if used improperly. There are also barrels that look like the kind Jeffrey Dahmer would fill with acid for dissolving bodies of dead drifters, but they only contain stagnant rainwater.

I'm looking for anything to eat — I feel like I've been in the building for days, trapped like that guy who had to saw off his own arm with a pocket knife and eat it. (I hope I am not played by James Franco.) I have four pieces of Bazooka bubble gum, but it's a decade stale, like chunks of limestone. The Bazooka Joe comics inside the gum are also horrible, some mid-Fifties anti-Chinese propaganda designed to sell Studebaker trucks. The walls of the warehouse may contain calcium or lime, if I could scrape the deposits from the walls, but I don't have a pocket knife.

It reminds me of a time I got stuck in that Twin Peaks town in Washington with a broken gas pedal in my car — probably told this story too many times — ended up at a laundromat, trying to buy a warm bottle of Grape Nehi with a two-dollar bill that no changing machine would cash. It was a hundred degrees out, and that show never addressed the few weeks of August when the greater Seattle area gets uncomfortably warm. Maybe Dale

Cooper has a thyroid problem. Too much coffee, gave him Epstein-Barr or something.

The warehouse continues on and on, a long corridor full of random boxes and discarded office furniture. There's a pile of Selectric typewriters that haven't been touched since Nixon was in office. I finally find the way out, the door where I first entered the building, and it's open. I have an old fire truck, not the long hook-and-ladder, but the small pickup truck the chief always rides around in, like an Army half-deuce, but painted a dull red. It's now much colder out, and snow is falling. I get in the truck, and when I crank the ignition, nothing happens. The lights are on, the battery is dead.

I walk from the warehouse in the snow — it's falling in big flakes, like there was an atomic bomb blast nearby and nuclear winter is starting. I'm thinking about all the evolutionary changes that will happen in animals after a nuclear winter: reptiles growing hair, mammals growing second sets of eyelids, people entering deep hibernation. Also, cartographers will be rich from having to redo every world map. I bet someone at the Thomas Guide company goaded the world leaders to start a war.

By the time I get to Ryan's Steakhouse, I realize there was no nuclear war. But the buffet is closed because of a health inspector raid, so I end up eating five Clark bars from a gas station for my late lunch.

* * *

The train tracks by my parents' old house were upgraded overnight, to a Disney-style monorail. Conrail and Amtrak didn't tell anyone they were doing it; they just installed everything quickly, and the trains now operate ten feet off the ground, whizzing by at like a hundred miles an hour. Everyone in town is upset for two reasons: they assume the whole thing was built with billions of dollars of tax money, and the elevated tracks have a clearance of nine feet, so most lifted 4x4s on monster tires won't fit under them, and nobody knows how to read the signs saying this, so dozens of trucks have smashed into the overpasses.

I walk the length of the track for about five miles in the middle of the night. The welders left big stainless steel canisters every dozen feet, tanks of liquid nitrogen or liquid hydrogen or something like that. I inspect the pressure gauge of each one, examine the needle on the dial to see if there's any remaining gas. I'm hoping one would still be full, and I could knock it over, break off the valve with a piece of scrap rebar, and turn the thing into a big rocket, a pressurized gas-propelled steel bullet the size of a person. But every tank is empty. One has about a half a PSI in it, and I crank open the valve, but it lets out nothing more then a gentle fart of gas, a tiny "pffft" and then nothing else.

This goes nowhere, burns up hours of my time, until I end up at a little diner in a building that was a Chevron gas station decades ago. It has six seats inside the area that used to be the mini-mart. The owner is boiling a curry or gravy or something in a 5,000-gallon underground gas tank he dug up and rigged with a bunch of Weber grills. The old awning from the station still stretches over the area where the pumps used to be. There are some plastic lawn chairs sitting on the patio, but they are covered in soot, and I don't eat outside on principle.

I spend the next hour talking to a guy from Utah about why Rush's best album is not *Vapor Trails*, but he isn't listening to me. He's playing with a new Nintendo portable thing, which doesn't have a screen or a controller or games. You press the side of it, and an annoying voice yells "MARIO!" or "LUIGI!" It costs $300. There's a limited-edition gold one you can only buy from Japan that says "POKEMON!" and costs ten times as much. I ask the guy why he doesn't buy one of those, and he starts crying.

I get a Diet Coke and walk back home. A guy in a wheelchair with no legs tells me if I don't give him my cell phone, he's going to kick my ass, and I start laughing. He tries to wheel up to me and smack me, but the pavement is all uneven and broken — the monorail installers completely screwed up the roads, and they would probably remain destroyed for years, long after the railroads are bankrupt and abandoned.

\* \* \*

An old-school seafood restaurant, which looks like it had been condemned in 1964, is hosting a poetry slam for Satanists. It's a Tuesday night, and I have to be up early the next morning, but I go anyway because I like fried cheese. A guy from an obscure death metal band is screaming verses about *The Sopranos* while pounding a bloody mary with like a pound of celery and vegetables and chicken nuggets sticking in it. He has a long, stringy beard, covered in tomato juice. I don't remember any of the lines of his poem except "turn Big Pussy towards hell."

I study the greasy plastic-coated food menu, which is as big as the tablets Moses hauled off the mountain. There are 400 kinds of seafood and a hamburger, but I hate seafood, so I get the burger, a basket of mozzarella sticks, and a side of lime ice cream. When my burger shows up, and it's covered with a gooey tar that smells like burned Velveeta cheese. The cheese sticks are pure black on the outside, frozen cheese on the inside. The ice cream is fine.

The waiter comes back to check on my drink and act like he cares. He looks like Karl Malden, but older. He tells us, "You know Tony Soprano got killed here? We have a plaque." I don't think much about it, but later remember the whole thing with the Journey song in the diner and the end of the episode cutting off, and regret I didn't ask the waiter more about it, or at least take a selfie.

* * *

Burt Lancaster is teaching me how to make a hoagie sandwich using Doritos instead of bread. (I can't remember exactly how he was doing it, something that involved plastic cling wrap and an extra-fat mayo they started selling in health food stores for some new fad diet.) This is an old Burt Lancaster, *Field of Dreams* old, a few years before he died. We're in a SoHo loft in a run-down mid-Eighties New York, like the one in *After Hours*, where Rosanna Arquette lived. Pictures of old Rochester carburetors in various states of disassembly cover the walls of the loft. I want to tell him I used to run a two-barrel Rochester on this Camaro I had when I was a kid, but it doesn't seem relevant.

I leave, walk down Prince Street, looking for this Korean grocery store that sells gourmet kimchi and still has Jolt cola. The clerk inside recognizes me, or thinks he does, asks me if I want to buy more bulk shrimp. I have no idea what he's talking about — I would never intentionally eat seafood. I find a case of Jolt, but it must be old, because the caustic liquid has partially dissolved the metal caps. I look at a bottle, and all the writing is in Korean, except for the logo and a warning sticker that says "NOT A LEGAL FOOD PRODUCT."

Can't tell what year it is — maybe the late Eighties, definitely pre-Giuliani. Lots of graffiti, no vegan cupcake shops on every corner. Some concept artists have jackhammered up an entire block of sidewalk on Lafayette, near the Great Jones Diner, and filled it with sand. Four dudes are buried up to their neck, like in that Bow Wow Wow video "I Want Candy" that is shown on MTV every hour in like 1982. A guy is playing what looks like a lute, but built out of a Mattel Intellivision and a bunch of Barbie dolls. I want to tell him the broken Barbie art thing is pretty played out, but without knowing the year, I don't really know if it is.

A strung-out college dropout selling cutout art books on a blanket in Astor Place starts yelling at me, telling me I need to take steroids and bulk up. I want to ask him if he's selling any detachable penises, but nobody ever gets that joke, not even King Missile fans.

*   *   *

Recursive dream: the base dream was something involving a Mormon conspiracy within the CERN supercollider, an LDS splinter faction trying to create a time portal to stop the invention of caffeine. Enter the second dream, wake up in my childhood home, with a stack of postal mail from friends I haven't talked to in twenty years. I'm answering the letters as fast as possible, writing about this conspiracy, trying to explain it on yellow legal notepads. I can't remember enough details to make the manifestos plausible, and my handwriting is borderline illegible, but I seal the letters shut in some *Minions* envelopes, walk to Kroger's at three in the morning to mail them, thinking about whether or not I should become a vegetarian or re-tile my bathroom. I wake up from both dreams on the floor of my actual bathroom, surrounded with legal pads covered in illegible scribbling, unable to determine if this is a third dream, and realize this is pretty much my life now.

# About the Author

Jon Konrath has written and published fifteen books, including *Summer Rain* and *Rumored to Exist*, and *Atmospheres*. He is the principal of Paragraph Line Books and editor of the literary journal *Paragraph Line*, and has written for many other zines and publications. He is also an inventor, computer programmer, photographer, sometimes podcaster, and owns several musical instruments he cannot play. He probably lives in Oakland. Find him online at rumored.com and paragraphline.com.